ALL THE BIRDS, SINGING

After the Fire, a Still Small Voice

Evie Wyld

All the Birds, Singing

PANTHEON BOOKS

NEW YORK

All rights reserved. Published in the United States by Pantheon Books, a division of Random House LLC, New York, and in Canada by Random House of Canada Limited, Toronto, Penguin Random House companies. Originally published in Great Britain by Jonathan Cape, an imprint of the Random House Group Limited, London, in 2013.

Pantheon Books and colophon are registered trademarks of Random House LLC.

A portion of this work first appeared in Granta's *Best of Young British Novelists* 4, Issue 123 (Spring 2013).

Library of Congress Cataloging-in-Publication Data
Wyld, Evie.
All the birds, singing : a novel / Evie Wyld.
    pages   cm
ISBN 978-0-307-90776-9 (hardback); ISBN 978-0-307-90777-6 (eBook)
1. Young women—Fiction. 2. Family secrets—Fiction. I. Title.
PR6123.Y43A696 2014   823'.92—dc23   2013033090

www.pantheonbooks.com

Jacket images: (wolf) NGS Image Collection/The Art Archive at Art Resource, N.Y.; (sheep) The New York Public Library/Art Resource, N.Y.
Jacket design by Joan Wong

Printed in the United States of America
First American Edition
2 4 6 8 9 7 5 3 1

for Roz, Roy and Gus

.

1

Another sheep, mangled and bled out, her innards not yet crusting and the vapours rising from her like a steamed pudding. Crows, their beaks shining, strutting and rasping, and when I waved my stick they flew to the trees and watched, flaring out their wings, singing, if you could call it that. I shoved my boot in Dog's face to stop him from taking a string of her away with him as a souvenir, and he kept close by my side as I wheeled the carcass out of the field and down into the woolshed.

I'd been up that morning, before the light came through, out there, talking to myself, telling the dog about the things that needed doing as the blackbirds in the hawthorn started up. Like a mad woman, listening to her own voice, the wind shoving it back down my throat and hooting over my open mouth like it had done every morning since I moved to the island. With the trees rattling in the copse and the sheep blaring out behind me, the same trees, the same wind and sheep.

That made two deaths in a month. The rain started to come down, and a sudden gust of wind flung sheep shit at the back of my neck so it stung. I pulled up my collar and shielded my eyes with my hand.

Cree-cra, cold, cree-cra, cold.

"What are you laughing at?" I shouted at the crows and lobbed a stone at them. I wiped my eyes with the back of my hand and breathed in and out heavily to get rid of the blood smell. The crows were silent. When I turned to look, five of them sat in a

1

row on the same branch, eyeing me but not speaking. The wind blew my hair in my eyes.

The farm shop at Marling had a warped and faded sign at the foot of its gate that read FREE BABY GUINEA PIGS. There was never any trace of the free guinea pigs and I had passed the point of being able to ask. The pale daughter of the owner was there, doing a crossword. She looked up at me, then looked back down like she was embarrassed.

"Hi," I said.

She blushed but gave me the smallest of acknowledgements. She wore a thick green tracksuit and her hair was in a ponytail. Around her eyes was the faint redness that came after a night of crying or drinking.

Normally the potatoes from that place were good, but they all gave a little bit when I picked them up. I put them back down and moved over to tomatoes, but they weren't any good either. I looked up out the window to where the farm's greenhouse stood and saw the glass was all broken.

"Hey," I said to the girl, who when I turned around was already looking at me, sucking the end of her pencil. "What happened to your greenhouse?"

"The wind," she said, taking her pencil to the side of her mouth just for a moment. "Dad said to say the wind blew it in."

I could see the glass scattered outside where normally they kept pots of ugly pink cyclamen with a sign that said THE JEWEL FOR YOUR WINTER GARDEN. Just black earth and glass now.

"Wow," I said.

"Things always get mad on New Year's Eve," said the girl in an older voice that surprised both of us. She blushed deeper and turned her eyes back to her crossword. In the greenhouse, the man who normally ran the shop sat with his head in his hands.

I took some oranges and leeks and lemons to the counter. I didn't need anything, the trip was more about the drive than the supplies. The girl dropped her pencil out of her mouth and started to count oranges, but wasn't sure of herself and started again a few times over. There was a smell of alcohol about her, masked by too much perfume. A hangover then. I imagined an argument with her father. I looked up at the greenhouse again, the man in it still with his head in his hands, the wind blowing through.

"Are there nine there?" she asked, and even though I hadn't counted as I put them in the basket I said yes. She tapped things into the till.

"Must be hard to lose the greenhouse," I said, noticing a small blue bruise at the girl's temple. She didn't look up.

"It's not so bad. We should have had an order over from the mainland, but the ferry's not going today."

"The ferry's not going?"

"Weather's too bad," she said, again in that old voice that embarrassed us both.

"I've never known that to happen."

"It happens," she said, putting my oranges in one bag and the rest in another. "They built the new boats too big so they aren't safe in bad weather."

"Do you know what the forecast is?"

The girl glanced up at me quickly and lowered her eyes again.

"No. Four pounds twenty please." She slowly counted out my money. It took two goes to get the change right. I wondered what new thing she'd heard about me. It was time to leave, but I didn't move.

"So what's with the free guinea pigs?"

The flush came back to her face. "They've gone. We gave them to my brother's snake. There were loads."

"Oh."

The girl smiled. "It was years ago."

"Sure," I said.

The girl put the pencil back in her mouth and her eyes fluttered back down to her crossword. She was just colouring in the white squares, it turned out.

In the truck, I found I had left the oranges in the shop. I looked out of my rear-view mirror at the smashed greenhouse and saw the man inside standing up with his hands on his hips looking at me. I locked the doors and drove away without the oranges.

It started to rain heavily, and I turned up the heating and put the wipers on full speed. We drove past the spot I usually stopped to walk Dog and he sat in the passenger seat and stared at me hard, and every time I turned to look at him he put his ears up, like we were mid-conversation and I was avoiding his look. "So what?" I said. "You're a dog." And then he turned around and looked out the window.

Midway home it caught up with me and I pulled over into the entrance to an empty field. Dog gazed stoically out the window, still and calm, and I pressed my thumb into the bridge of my nose to try and take away the prickling, clung on to the skin of my chest with the nails of my other hand to melt away that old thudding ache that came with losing a sheep, a bead of blood landing in an open eye. I cried drily, honking and with my mouth open, rocking the truck and feeling something grappling around inside me getting no closer to coming out. *Have a good cry*, it was the kind of thing Mum'd say to a triplet in the hope a visit to the hospital wasn't necessary. Like the time Cleve fell out of a tree and cried it out, and we found out later he had a broken arm. But there was nothing good in my crying—it prevented me from breathing, it hurt. I stopped once my nose began to bleed, cleaned it up with the shammy I used on the days the windows were iced on the inside and drove home, calmly. On the Military Road near to the turning home, some teenagers fondled about at the bus stop. When they saw me coming one of the boys pretended to put something in his mouth, another mounted him from behind and humped him while he mimed throwing a lasso. The girls laughed and gave me the finger. As I rounded the corner the boy with the lasso dropped his trousers and showed his white arse.

I put a pot of coffee down on the stove harder than I needed to. "Fucking kids," I said to Dog, but he had his back to me and wasn't listening.

I slammed the fridge and leant my head against it. Stupid to have become so comfortable. The fridge hummed back in agreement. Stupid to think it wouldn't all fall to shit. That feeling I'd had when I first saw the cottage, squat and white like a chalk pebble at the black foot of the downs, the safety of having no one nearby to peer in at me—that felt like an idiot's lifetime ago. I felt at the side of the fridge for the axe handle.

My sleeve was brown where some of the dead sheep had leaked onto it and I took my jumper off and rubbed the spot with soap in the downstairs bathroom. I smelled like billy goat but the idea of a full wash with the cold deep in my shoulders didn't interest me, so I just splashed under my armpits. My hands clenched and unclenched to warm up, the right one aching and clicking in the way that it did in damp weather where the bones hadn't knitted back together.

I smoothed back the skin of my face in the mirror. The last fringe I'd given myself had been an inch too short and I looked like a mad person. I found a blooded thumbprint below my ear.

I lit a cigarette, holding it with my lips and clasping my hands together in front of me to tense my arms as I inhaled to check the muscle tone and it was still there even if I hadn't sheared in a couple of months. *Strong lady.* I watched the smoke snake its way out of my mouth and disappear in the cold air. The coffee pot began its death rattle, and I moved to take it off the hob. I still had a fear of the thing exploding.

Out the kitchen window, the flash of a windscreen across the valley. Don in his Land Rover. I spat my cigarette into the sink, ran the water over it, and then bolted out into the yard to get the wheelbarrow, and Dog nipped me on the back of the knee for running. I huffed up to the top of the drive, the barrow squeaking to buggery, and stood, blocking the road. Don pulled up and cut the engine. Midge stayed patiently in the passenger's seat eyeballing Dog with her pink tongue lolling out.

"Christ alive. You're making my balls shrink," Don said as he swung himself out of the truck. It was sleeting and I only wore my singlet. He passed a glance at me that I rolled off my shoulders. "You look like shit. Not sleeping?"

"I'm fine." I nodded to the wheelbarrow. Don looked at it.

"What's that you got there?"

"Another dead ewe. Reckon it's those kids."

He looked at me. Our breath puffed white between us. He shook his head.

"What's a kid want to go and do that for?"

"Why does anyone do anything? Bored and shitful."

Dog jumped up at Midge sitting in the truck and barked at her while she looked back coolly.

"No," said Don, "can't blame everything on the kids. Even if some of them's vicious little buggers.

"What's gone on here then?" he asked the dead sheep, bending forward and taking a closer look; his hands were on his hips. It was very cold. I folded my arms over my chest and tried to look comfortable.

"I found her this morning out by the woods."

"By the woods?"

I nodded.

He shook his head and walked around the wheelbarrow. "She's dead all right."

"Oh really? You a vet?"

Don narrowed his eyes at me.

I cleared my throat. "These kids . . ."

Don tipped his cap up off his eyes and looked at me. "Good night last night—you shoulda come down the pub last night like I said."

Here we go, I thought. "Not my sort of place, Don." I pictured the men who would be there, leaning up against the bar and talking in low voices, their eyes flicking up when a woman walked by. The same sort as the three who had showed up in the first week, whistling farmer-wants-a-wife. Don was different. I'd called on him with my first breech birth and he'd come with me, calmly sewed the prolapsed innards back into the ewe and saved her triplets, poured me a drink and said lightly, *All gotta learn one way or the other.*

Still, he could go on for ever.

"Three years. You haven't been out to the pub once."

This was a lie. I'd been there once, but Don liked to say it so much that he never listened when I told him.

"You show up, arm in a sling, looking like a lesbian or a hippy or something, and you move in and we don't have many of either of those round here. You're not careful, they're going to use stories about you to scare the nippers."

I shifted my weight, feeling the cold setting into my jawbone.

"It's a lonely enough job sheep farming without putting yourself in isolation."

I blinked at Don and there was a long pause. Dog whined. He'd heard it all before as well.

7

"So what killed my sheep then?" was all I could say.

Don sighed and squinted at the sheep. He looked about a hundred in the morning light; the age spots on his cheeks were livid. "Mink might tear a sheep up, after she's dead. Or a fox." He lifted the ewe's head to take a look at the eyes. "Eyes are gone," he said; "could be something killed her and then everything else took their pickings." He lifted the head higher and looked underneath where her ribs made a cave. He frowned. "But I've never seen anything round here flense an animal like that."

I patted the pocket of my trousers, where I kept my cigarettes, then I touched Dog on the top of his greasy head. A crow called out, *Caaa-creee, caaa-creee.* Midge stood up on her seat and we all looked over the fence at the dark trees there.

"Just tell those kids if you see them, and anyone else who wants to hear about it, that if I catch anyone near my sheep I'll shoot them."

I turned the wheelbarrow around and started walking back down the hill towards home.

"Yep," said Don, "happy new year to you too."

8

2

We are a week from the end of the job in Boodarie. I'm in the shower at the side of the tractor shed watching the thumb-sized redback that's always sat at the top of the shower head. She hasn't moved at all except to raise a leg when I turn on the tap, like the water's too cold for her.

The day has been a long and hot one—the tip of March, and under the crust of the galvo roof the air in the shearing shed has been thick like soup, flies bloating about in it. I'm low on shampoo, but I use a good slug of it, and feel the suds run down my dips and crevices, the water cooling off my lower back where the scars get hot and throb with the sweat. Above me, beyond the redback, is a fast blackening sky—the night comes quickly here, not like in the city where you could spend all night at work and not notice its difference to the day, other than the slowing off of customers. The first stars are bright needles, and in the old Moreton Bay fig that hangs over the tractor shed and drops nuts on the roof while I sleep, a currawong and a white galah are having it out; I can hear the blood-thick bleat of them. A flying fox goes overhead and just like that the smell of the place changes and night has settled in the air. Someone moves outside the pallet-board screen of the shower and I still my hands in my hair.

"Greg?" I call, but no answer. I turn the tap off to listen. The redback sets down her leg. "Greg?" The suds are still thick in my hair and they keep up a crackle in my earholes. I think of being found alone and taken away, back there, tied up and left to rot in the long dry grasses. There is a smell of fat and eggs frying. Someone steps quietly around the shower. It could be any of the team, could be Alan who is getting deaf these days, looking for electrical tape or kerosene or batteries or rags. But it is not, that much is clear from the change in the air. "Greg?" I am less than 150 kilometers from Otto's, the closest I've been since I left, but still, in seven months, I've travelled up and down the country and even if he has a nose like a bloodhound, I've covered my tracks. *I've covered my tracks*, I mouth.

The pallet to my right darkens, and through a punched-out knot in the grain of the wood, an eye appears, and I back away from it, my voice gone.

"I know about you," says the eye. "You don't fool me; I know about you and what you've done," it says and the voice is thick and sticky and there's the smell of rotten eggs and lanolin together and whisky and unwashed places.

I've covered my tracks, it's been seven months and I covered my tracks, but my heart is beating fast, and I have to put up my hand to the wall to steady myself. The spider reacts, turns in a small circle, settles again. The eye twitches, and I think of driving my thumbnail right into it, but I can't bring myself to touch it, and there is nothing else sharp to poke with. The eye slides up and down, the iris a milky blue.

"I know what you're about," says the eye. It disappears and the shadow moves away. My heart drums. I look through the knot in the wood and see Clare staggering off in the direction of the shearing shed. He's been away the week, and he has found something out.

I bolt from the shower without washing out the suds, round the side of the shed to my sleeping quarters. I pull on pants, shorts and a singlet and then I begin stuffing everything else into my backpack. *If you were so sure he'd never find you,* says my head,

10

why are you so prepared to leave, why do all your belongings fit in a backpack? Everything is in there except my shears, which I left on the bench next to the wool table, to sharpen in the morning. And the carapace of a cicada that Greg gave me last month when he asked if I'd go to the Gold Coast with him once the job was done. I hold it in my palm and it vibrates with my pulse.

"Just spend a month at the water. Fishing, swimming, drinking beer," he'd said. "Get the dust off us before the next job."

I put the skin back down on the ledge and go to find Greg in the dinner hall.

Almost everyone has gathered for tea, and I scan the bench for Clare, but he's not there. I sit down next to Greg, who is talking to Connor about boat engines, and I try to make it clear I want to talk to him by putting my hand on his shoulder. He squeezes my thigh under the table but doesn't turn around, too involved with his conversation.

". . . corroded so far, it broke through and dropped down into the bilge," he says, and Connor is drinking from his can and he says,

"Yep. That's just the way she'll go—people forget." His voice becomes high-pitched and incredulous. "As far as an engine is concerned—water's your enemy."

"Yep," says Greg and I shift about next to him. I don't want anyone else to know there's a problem.

"You right?" asks Greg, distracted by my fidgeting.

"I need to talk to you," I say quietly.

Greg looks at me a moment, takes a swig of his drink and snakes his arm around my back.

"Can we go somewhere?"

"Tea's coming out."

"Yes but . . ."

"Whisper it."

11

I lean closer to him. People assume we are having some sort of moment I suppose, and no one could be less interested. A grey steak arrives in front of me and trays of boiled potatoes get passed down the line.

My mouth goes dry. "Have you seen Clare yet?"

"His truck's back, he'll be around somewhere. Why—what's he owe you?"

"Nothing. I just— Look, can we go to the Gold Coast?"

He gives me a hopeless look, like he doesn't know what on earth is the matter with the woman. "Yeah. I suggested it. What, are you having a stroke or something?" He puts six large potatoes on his plate, passes the tray, which I pass on to Stuart on the other side of me.

"I mean now. Can we just hop in the truck and go now?"

"Why? What's happened?"

"Nothing's happened. I just want to go now."

Greg looks confused. "Well, so do I, but we've got to finish the job."

"Why?"

Greg is chewing on a lump of steak. "Why? Because these are me mates, I'm not leaving them a man down. Besides, we go early, we don't get the bonus—it's just a week we've got left. Not long." He swallows and reaches for one of the rolls that sit in the centre of the table. "Sid," he shouts, "is this bread still made with the arse flour?" Sid doesn't reply and Greg shrugs and mops his plate.

"Can you just trust me that we need to leave now?" I say.

He puts his bread down. "Why do we *need* to leave now? What is the difference? You rob a bank?"

I open my mouth to speak, but there is nothing I can tell him.

"See," he says, picking up his fork again, "there's no problem. Everything is simple. It's just hot is all, we'll be at the Coast in no time."

12

Another tray starts to come down, with sausages on it. When I pass this to Stuart he looks at me strangely.

"No snag for you?" he says.

"What?"

"On Jenny Craig or something?"

I ignore him, but Greg notices too, and waves the sausages back. "Wait wait wait, if she's not eating I'll have hers," and he spears two extra.

"Why do you get the extra?" asks Stuart.

"Because she's my woman."

"What? That's not right."

"Fair dinkum," Denis says from down the end. "She's his woman, means the snags pass on to him."

I wish I had taken the sausages.

I have until the end of tea to convince him.

Greg has eaten my steak, and two large bowls of tinned fruit cocktail with the shining red cherries and the pale cubes of melon are distributed along the table.

Someone barks, "What, no ice cream?" and Sid tosses a couple of bricks of it, the kind you cut with a pallet knife and which are bright yellow like cheese, and Connor hacks off a two-inch slice and dumps a ladle of fruit salad on top.

"Love it when the ice cream mixes with the syrup," he says loudly to anyone who wants to know, and then he picks out the red cherries one by one with his fingers, his pinkie held up high, and lines them up at the side of his dish, "but those little fuckers can get bent."

Clare appears in the doorway with the night behind him. The strip lighting in the shed makes him look like he glows. He holds on to the door frame and scans the long table. I wait for his eyes to settle on me, and when they do I see a look of pleasure on his face that I recognise. I am trapped. Greg's thigh pumps blood

13

next to mine. Connor scrapes the bottom of his dish with his spoon and Steve, next to him, flicks one of the red cherries so it darts onto Stuart's lap. Stuart gives Steve the finger without looking up from his bowl. Alan at the top of the table is reading the paper and is not interested. He drinks his beer. And in all of it, Clare looks at me and I know I'm done, I know the end has come. He enters the room and walks slowly past me. I try not to crane to follow him, I try not to anticipate his next move. He puts a hand on Greg's shoulder and bends down to him, and I tense myself for the end. Greg looks up and Clare hands him a Violet Crumble and Greg's face opens out into a smile.

"Good man," says Greg. "Now I don't have to get involved with this horse shit," he says, nodding at the fruit salad and pinching open the purple wrapper as he does it. Clare ambles on by, saying nothing, just giving me a sidelong glance. Greg breaks the end off his bar and hands it to me. While Greg is turned away from me, I crumble it to dust under the table.

I pick up my shears from the shed, and do not think about what will happen next. The shed smells good. Sweat and dung, lanolin and turps. I can't imagine being away from it. A possum scratches on the tin roof. I walk slowly back to my quarters, stand for a moment in the dark where I can see the warm slice of light in the dinner shed, where I have a side view of Greg, who is laughing, who brings a beer to his lips, who drinks, who puts it down and wipes his mouth with the back of his hand. I bite the tip of my tongue and I try to think of some last-minute plan that can stop this. Nothing comes and I turn away and follow my feet back to my quarters.

Clare is lying on my bed with his boots on, smoking a roll-up. I stop in the doorway, but he's heard me coming and he's ready with a toothy smile for me. I stay in the doorway

14

wondering if I can turn around, walk back to the woolshed, hide under a fleece.

"Know where I was all week?" he asks, swinging his legs off my bed and standing up. "Come in out of the doorway, love," he says, "you look like a prostitute." He grins wider, if that is possible. He blows smoke out and it fogs the air between us. "Planning a trip?" he says, in the voice of someone off the TV. He kicks my backpack gently. There is so much excitement in his voice.

"Ben tipped me off about the posters—pictures of you plastered all around the place down there. Did you know that? I had to go and see for myself—but they're you all right." He pulls from his back pocket a scored and folded piece of paper. He unfolds it slowly, chuckling to himself, and holds it up to show me. There I am in black and white sitting on my pink pony doona cover, smiling for the camera. There's a stuffed bear on my lap and my hands are digging into it, not that you can see my hands, not that you can see the bear or the doona cover or the old man taking the photograph or the dog guarding me outside. You can only see my face, the smile for the camera. In capital letters it says MISSING at the top and I catch the words "granddaughter . . . danger to herself," at the bottom, but I can't read it all because things have gone dark.

"I rang the number, Jake, and you know what I found out?"

"I don't know what you're talking about. He's not my grandfather."

"Oh, I know all that. That poor old bloke, 'Otto.' We had a good long chat. I went to see him on his farm, just a pen of dead sheep, and all he can talk about is how you killed his dog and how you took his money and he was only trying to take you off the street. Said you took everything that was dear to him, took his truck even, poor old cracker couldn't get into town, had to rely on the Salvos to come once a week with groceries until he

15

got his old banger working. Saw what you did to that too, smashed it up pretty bad."

"I didn't, I just—"

"I saw it. The old bugger cried when he talked about his dog."

"I just—"

"Shhh," Clare says, but loudly. He gets up off the bed in one fluid movement and walks towards me slowly, takes my forearms where they hang limply by my sides. He moves me over to stand in front of the workbench and he leans on me, crotch heavy.

"You might have fooled them, but you don't fool me."

My mouth waters. I look over at the doorway. What would happen if Greg appeared in there now?

"What you've got, is you've got two options here. Maybe I'd be persuaded to keep my mouth shut." Clare's breath is hot fudge on the side of my face. He whispers in a way that sounds like soon he'll be shouting. "You can show me some of what you've shown everyone else at the Hedland . . ." My heart tumbles around my body. A stupid part of me thinks, *He might not say anything*, and is quieted by the part of me that knows it will not end, and I cannot stay here. "Little bit of affection—I'm not asking for much—I wouldn't fuck a mate's lay—maybe just the mouth." And I can see exactly how it will all be, the back of the throat, the hair grasped in a ponytail, and the words he will say while he does it, and then afterwards how it will only be worse, how he will be rid of me either way, and with a flourish. "Or," he says, trailing his finger along the outer curve of my breast, "or I can let old Otto know where to find you, and the police." He starts to unbutton my shorts, and he tugs my singlet out from them, and puts a hand down, scrabbling with his fingers to get beneath my underwear. "I won't even have to tell Greg, they'll do it for me." He scrapes a finger over my crotch, and like a mechanical game at the fairground, something is triggered and I punch him in the jaw with my right and he goes down, out cold and bleeding on the floor.

I cannot do up my shorts because my hand crunched badly against Clare's face, and it has turned into a meat fist, throbbing and swollen.

I leave the room without looking back at him, but I can hear him shifting about in the dust and a wet groan comes from him. I am fairly sure that I have broken his jaw.

3

I watched Don drive down into the valley in the last of the light, stayed there with the wheelbarrow in the sleet, with Dog sheltering behind my legs, until he'd disappeared over the crest of the hill to the other side where he lived. My boots made a crumping sound as I walked back down the path to the woolshed. There were times I felt how unnatural I was in the place, the way my skin still stung at the cold, the way the insides of my nostrils and the back of my throat prickled. The smell of wet wool and rain-dampened sheep shit were aliens to the dust-dry smell of the carpet sheep in their wide red spaces back home. The way the land seemed to be watching me, feeling my foreignness in it, holding its breath until I passed by. I'd asked Mum once, *What kind of Aussies are we? Did we come over on the boats, or did someone take us here later on?* Mum'd looked up from where she was struggling to get the triplets bare white arses into undies, and blew a hank of hair out of her face. "I've been here for ever, darl," she said and swatted one of the kids on the legs to try and get them to keep still. I'd never pushed further than that.

I tried not to look too hard into the trees which were black even in the morning, but from the corner of my eye I saw something flicker and I started, thinking the trees were on fire but there was nothing, just some slight movement in the wind. The sheep coughed and bleated. I parked the wheelbarrow in the woolshed and closed the door. My teeth chattered and when I got inside the house, I pulled on my coat and sat on the sofa. Dog climbed up damply next to me.

I hadn't called in over a month. The last time no one was in and I let it ring out thinking about the phone in the front room, how the sound of it made the magpies lift off the veranda and then settle back down. How the air moved with the ringer, the air that smelled of washing left too long in the machine, of three young boys and their socks and undies, the long-gone deep-fat fryer whose smell, as I remembered it, still soaked into the walls. Mum's back-door cigarettes that we weren't allowed to know about, and somewhere from an open window, the smell of sugar and eucalyptus, the hot breath of the trees.

I dialled the code to withhold my number and tapped in the long sequence that I knew by heart. It took me through the tones and silences of connection to home. It would barely be daybreak there, but Mum was an early riser—always had been. It rang out twice and I stroked the arm of the sofa to hear the sound of Mum's voice.

"Hello, 635?" she said and waited. "Hello? Hello hello?"

A sigh, from her chest which sounded shallow and wheezy. It would have been her birthday the week before. Seventy-two.

"Iris!" she called. "It's doing that thing again." A thickness in her throat, a cold or an allergy. My sister's voice, muffled, maybe from upstairs.

"*Just hang up the phone, Ma, for Christ's sake!*"

"Well, what's wrong with the phone though?"

Iris closer now, down the stairs and entering the room. "How the hell should I know." The clunk of the phone being taken out of my mother's deeply veined hands and into Iris's heavily ringed fingers. "Hello?" My sister's voice, sharp like always, edged with being the eldest. She listened to my silence. "I dunno, Mum, maybe you've got a pervert after you."

19

On the receiver's journey through the air into the cradle, I heard the beginning of a butcher bird's song, *ceecaw-ceeceecaw*— and the line went dead. Back in my living room with the electric heater on and smelling of burnt dust, I finished the song, whistling. *Pwee pwee pwee pwee pwee pwee pwee pwee pwee pwee pweeee.* Dog raised his ears at the sound but it wasn't that unusual to him. I started a set of push-ups, but halfway through lay down and stared at the ceiling.

I made some coffee and drank it. After some time had passed, I laid out my paperwork on the kitchen table and worked through it. When that was done I let Dog out to pee, but stayed in the doorway in my socks. I put the paperwork away and folded myself up on the sofa with a book that I held unopened on my lap. The wind moved through the trees, down the chimney and into the front room where it waved through the top sheet of a newspaper.

With the night outside I closed the curtains in the kitchen and put on the radio loud enough to drown out the skittering noises of leaves moving up the stone path. The only programme I could get was the soccer results. I listened to the names of places while I made sardines on toast. Wigan. What was Wigan like? I had a pretty strong sense of it just from the name, and it made me glad that I was not there. I fed a sardine to Dog and it made him sneeze.

The sitting room was cold and so I ate under a blanket. I didn't look out the window at the dark, but I felt it there.

Burnley, three; Middlesbrough, nil.

When I could find no further reasons for not being in bed, I turned the radio off and whistled tunelessly and loudly on my way up the stairs. On the landing a feather fluttered in a draught. I brushed my teeth and must've scraped over a mouth ulcer, because when I spat there was an impressive amount of blood. I washed it away and blew my nose and then rolled on an old T-shirt to sleep in. Dog collected himself at the foot of the bed, and we stared at each other a moment or two before I checked the hammer under my pillow and turned off the light. I closed my eyes so that I wasn't staring into the dark, and I tried not to take any notice of the sounds that felt unfamiliar, even though I'd heard them a million times before. A sheep's cough had always sounded just like a person's. A fox was being made love to somewhere in the woods and her shrieks cut straight into my room.

I fell asleep, because I woke up from a dream where I saw myself opening the bathroom door and finding all of my sheep in there, looking silently back at me. There was no colour or light in the sky, so it wasn't past five. There was something sick in the air, like someone had lit a scented candle to mask a bad smell. The house was still. Dog stood by the closed door, looking at the space underneath, his hackles up and his legs straight and stiff, his tail rigid, pointing down. And then one creak, on the ceiling, like someone walked there. I held my breath and listened past the blood thumping in my ears. It was quiet and I pulled the covers up under my chin. The sheets chafed loudly against themselves. Dog stayed fixed on the door. A small growl escaped him.

My fingernails dug into my palms.

On the wall behind me came a noise like someone drawing a nail from the ceiling to the top of my bed's headboard and stopping there, one straight smooth and slow line. Dog slunk over to the bed and growled long and low. I lay still, felt every muscle beat in time with my heart; my back throbbed now. I had the feeling that I had bled onto the bedsheets, that if I moved my back would stick to the material and pull at my skin.

21

I thought to myself, *Rats, there's rats in the walls or mice, the smaller ones with the soft little brown bodies, that is all it is, or a bit of old timber releasing air, or cracking, the temperature outside has dropped in the night, it is making it crack and the mice are scurrying around, scratching about, or it is the Rayburn's pipe, doing its thing—the wind has changed direction.*

An underwater stillness, no wind or rain, not even a small owl, just a thick blanket of silence. I shut my eyes, and felt the mattress creak as Dog loped up on it, and weaved himself between my feet. The room settled and I counted heartbeats. There was a quiet crackle then silence again.

And then a sound like someone driving a car into a tree, a crack and a slam that echoed, and then like hands slapping fast on the wall, and I stood up on my bed and lowed like a bull, clutching a pillow in front of me, and holding the hammer up as if there was someone to hit with it. Dog snapped at the air around him like it was full of flies.

In the quiet that followed, Dog started to howl. I lumped off the bed and hit the light switch. The door was now open, flush with the wall like someone had stood there, blocking the doorway, observing. The corridor beyond it was dark and longer than I remembered it.

"Fuck! You!" I shouted into the corridor, breathing deep between each word, and around the words I thought I could hear a whisper of someone speaking back to me. Dog stopped howling, let out a moan and ran into the darkness of the hallway. Nothing showed up at the end of the hall, just the window, and outside, the night. I took my jeans from the floor and pulled them on as I moved down the corridor to the stairway.

The light switch at the top of the stairs was not where it should have been, so I ploughed into the dark and down to the kitchen where I found the light already on and Dog sitting under the table with drool coming out of him and puddling on the floor.

We went out the door and got into the car, started the engine, and I drove with my hands shaking against the steering wheel. I was going to drive straight into town, straight to the police station and bang on the door, but as my heart slowed down, so did my driving, and I parked in the driveway of a field in sight of the lights of town, turned the engine off. Dog curled in the footwell of the passenger seat and shook, his eyes black and round. I rested my head on the steering wheel and breathed in and out until the still and the quiet became natural and Dog crawled from his footwell and let me rub his ears. "We'll be okay," I said to him and he looked at me. "We've got options. We're smart—right? Right?"

We watched the light draw through the sky and a barn owl on her final patrol who broke up the dawn, a lone swimmer in an empty sea.

Back home, the kitchen was just the same, the stove bleating out when the wind flew over its pipes. Standing at the door of my bedroom, my bed was normal. There was no bad smell, there was no bad nothing.

I pulled the bed sheets straight and laid the blanket over the top. Just on the edge of the white coverlet was a black mark, like I'd trailed it in the ashes of a fire. I wiped at the smudge with the flat of my hand and it faded. The wall above the bedhead also had a smudge but this one was more of a print. I must have leant against it when I was standing and yelling, and left a hand-print clear and black with the fingers spread so that the webs of skin between them must have pulled and ached. But the hand was smaller than my own; I rubbed it off with toilet paper and spit.

4

There is a moment that I see things change with Greg. Waking up with him in my bed becomes something that happens, and the small time we have before work is as important as the rest of it. We do not watch each other sleep like they do in the movies; if one of us wakes first, we wake the other with a rough shake: "Hey, wake up."

This is not the time for sleeping. We don't lie in silence and stare at each other either—we talk like magpies, gabbling out the words like we're in competition with each other. I do push-ups while he talks; he rests his feet on my shoulders, and I move them up and down for him. He tells me about his father, who is dead, but who could eat a whole watermelon with just a spoon and the top cut off like a boiled egg. "Heh, he was the fattest fucker. And proud of it—some doctor tried to tell him to lose weight, and he said, 'What would I be then? I would just be Joe, I wouldn't be Fat Joe any more, and who would care when I died?' Heh. Fat fucker."

And when it's my turn, I do sit-ups, which are easier to talk around, and Greg plants his feet on mine to spot me. He never mentions it is strange, he never says, *Careful you'll get too manly.* I tell him the in-between bits of my life, the bits that are available. Learning to shear, my friend Karen, and further back, the sharks, the bush.

In the morning, Sid finds out weevils have made it into the flour.

"I don't particularly mind," he says. "I'm just saying in case anyone has an aversion to having the buggers in the bread." There is silence while the table takes this in, and it is broken by a shout from Alan by the side of the woolshed.

Something has taken a bite out the side of one of the rams. He's not dead, just looks like someone tore past him and took a chunk out. Flies swarm the wound. Connor shoots the ram, while we all stand around. The animal twitches.

"Just nerves firing," Denis says to me, like I am a hysterical woman who needs comforting. But I'm thinking how quick it was and what a mercy. One second horribly wounded, feeling flies lay their eggs in your flesh and watching the currawong circle, and the next, in a flash, all is safe. I will learn to fire a gun, I think, they are the answer.

Alan stands next to me. "Come on," he says, "we'll have a drive around, see if we can find a feral dog or something." Connor and Clare move the ram's body out of the pen, the rest of the sheep look on. There is no way of telling what they think.

In the truck I'm alone with Alan. This has not happened before, and he's got something he wants to say. He keeps coughing into his fist and then looking over at me. There is nothing for miles, nothing but that desert heat-wobble, and now and then a rabbit, which Alan picks off and we scoop up as we drive past. It's not silent exactly in the truck, but all we say are things like "Over there," and "Bloody got him," and "A little bit bloody closer."

After an hour, when I'm thinking about how much time is wasting and how far ahead of me the rest of the team will be, Alan tips the bullets out of the rifle and sighs.

"There's nothing bloody else out here," he says and then he turns to me. "I don't normally bloody interfere in anyone's business," he says, and I grip the wheel. "But I've been meaning to say, I think it's not a bad thing you and Greg." I wait for *but* . . . and it doesn't come. "You're both good bloody blokes, and the

25

thing is that I've known Greg a while and he's a good bloke." The truck is heating up and I wonder if I should start to drive home or if starting the engine now would be rude. "And you're a good bloke, and I reckon together, two good blokes is a good thing." Alan is red in the face and I wonder why he is putting us through this. "Thing is, what I'm bloody getting at, is that you gotta ignore the bloody loonies in life, and listen there are one or two of them in the team. Not bad blokes all in all, but . . . lonely blokes maybe."

"I'm not sure—"

"Listen, just don't be bothered by Clare is what I'm bloody getting at. He's a lunatic, a good bloke, but a lunatic, and he's messed himself up with the business with the kid . . ." Alan shakes his head. "Arthur's mum sent a letter—he's trying to learn to write with the other hand—lot of good that'll do him, kid can barely read. Anyhow."

"Has he said something?"

"Look, it's not even about that."

"What did he say?" I keep my voice steady and my eyes on the heat-wobble in the distance.

"I'm not interested," says Alan. "Look, I'm not interested in what my team have done before. Hell, I've bloody got a past, we've all got pasts—you want to find one of us who chooses to be out here without a past, I'd bloody pay to see that. Denis—he's been doing this his whole bloody life—fifty years of this. You think there isn't something he's getting away from?"

He looks at me and I can tell he wants me to know something, and for a second I think, *What did you do, Alan?*

"What I'm saying is," he carries on, "Clare can be a whinging bitch. He's a good bloke, but a whinging bitch. And I don't take any notice of him or of the past. Let's not forget Clare and Greg are best mates. He's just acting like a prick because he's jealous, but he can't admit to that because, well—he's a prick. It's been hard on him being roustabout. But what I'm saying is maybe talk to Greg about it—get him to go out for a night with Clare, just the two of them. Might quieten him down a bit. Clare'll be off for a week soon—that'll help too."

"I'm not forcing Greg to hang out with me," I say. My face is hot and there's an anger I wasn't expecting.

"I'm not saying that—I'm just saying if we're all living together like we are—might be the . . . political thing to do." He sniffs loudly. This has gone further than he wanted it to.

In the silence he holds the rabbits up by the ears, out the open window of the truck. Each of them is cleanly done behind the shoulder. He holds them high in the air, breathing through an open mouth and watching beads of thick blood drop from them onto the orange dirt.

"Was thinking to take 'em back for Sid, thinking he might make a bloody casserole or something." A fly settles on the wound of one of the rabbits. He leans back and throws the dead rabbits in a high arc away from the truck. "He'd only make 'em taste of bloody arseholes anyway," he says, and we drive back to the station. I itch to get back to work.

"Catch a shark?" Greg asks and I smile at him. I don't feel like speaking. Clare keeps his back to me.

At smoko, Sid comes in, bright red and snarling. "Right, which one of you useless fucktards did it?" he says, standing at the top of the table. I look down the line of men, trying to work out what has been done and who has done it. Clare is smirking behind his moustache.

"What's the bloody drama now?" asks Alan, who has just come in. Sid drags his glare away from the table.

"Come and see for yourself," he says and when he moves to the back where the kitchen is set up, we all stand up and follow.

Everyone crowds around the flour barrel, and when Sid takes the lid off, there's a bum print there.

"It's not fucking funny!" shouts Sid above everyone's honking laughter. Greg doubles over like he's in pain.

"Well, we can rule one person out," says Alan, wiping his eyes. He points to the edge of the bum print, where you can make out another print. "Culprit's got balls at least."

"Up to Boonderie next week," Alan announces at tea. "Hot as a bloody dog's gut up there."

It's as far north as I've been since leaving, but the people of Hedland won't mix with the people of Boonderie. Still, my mouth goes dry and I scull a beer to dampen myself down.

Sid makes bread out of the weevily bum flour, and it sits, turning to rock, in the centre of the table. No one will touch it, not even Stuart, not even with a fork.

The light is out and Greg has his large thumbs in the dips of my pelvis, and the shed is hot and dry. I feel out of myself tonight, like my bones have become too heavy for my flesh. The heat gets itself in under the metal roof during the day and it stays there at night, making the spiders sleepy. I loop my fingers in Greg's hair, to let him know I'm still paying attention and to try and remind myself to keep focused. A frog is creaking outside, and so maybe soon there'll be rain hammering the roof. Sometimes when it rains, which is not often, it feels like the drumming will knock the spiders off and onto my bed.

The frog stops, and there is a cool breeze that swims into the shed, like the kind of wind rain makes when it's on its way down. Greg sighs, I remember where I am, and grasp harder at his hair. Something large and black darts in the doorway, skitters along the far wall and under the workbench, and I bounce up in bed, knocking Greg in the face with my groin and taking a clump of his hair with me. "The fuck?" he says, holding his face with both hands.

"There's something in here," I whisper, though whispering is pointless against Greg's noise.

"What something?" He examines his palm for blood from his nose and then feels for the spot I ripped his hair from. "Fuckin' needed that," he says.

"Under the workbench, something big." He looks up at me, his expression changes.

"How big?"

I'm feeling under the bed for the hammer. I can't find it in the dark. Greg lifts himself off the bed and gives his head a small shake to clear it. He goes lightly over to the switch and turns it on. The strobing of the strip light does nothing but throw shadows.

"Like a big dog."

The strobe settles, but there are still shadows and places to hide. The workbench is covered by a blue oilcloth which hangs down and hides the space under it. Greg picks up the metal pipe that leans against the wall. I'm glad that he kept his underwear on—I think, *This would be so much worse if he was naked.* I have made his nose bleed, but he ignores it, lets it flow down on to his lip, while he holds the pole with both hands like a cricket bat. He treads carefully and slowly towards the workbench, his eyes dart around finding new shadows. The hair on the back of my neck prickles. I try not to think of Kelly, or picture Otto outside holding a gun, watching. Holding his cut-throat. He will shoot Greg then he will do me slowly; Kelly will snap at the air by my face as she watches me die. He will cut off my hand and give it to her as a prize. *Kelly is dead,* I think, but the thought is not a comfort.

I take the corner of the oilskin in my fingers, look to Greg who raises his arms, ready to strike if something runs out. He tells me with a nod of three to lift it, and I make my own countdown and jerk the cover up. Under the workbench, there is nothing. Greg lets his arms fall at his sides and the metal pipe clangs on the floor.

"Jesus," he says, "if you weren't in the mood you just had to say."

I look at him to see if this is a joke, but I can't tell.

Later, when he sleeps next to me, I get up out of bed and, careful not to wake him, I pull on a shirt and some shorts, and leave the shed. It is cooler out; I concentrate on breathing, sucking the cool air in, blowing the hot air out. The night sky is crisp with stars and I sit on the fence, listening to the cicadas and the night birds, the bandicoots and rats and all the live things that are out there, breathing with me. Not far away, the sheep are a dense and silent cluster. I feel the pull of being alone, of answering to no one, the safety of being unknown and far away. I sense a small movement behind me and turn just in time to see a shadow in the doorway of the shed. But it's Greg, I know his shape, and he doesn't want me to have seen him, and I don't want him to have seen me, and when I get back to bed an hour later, he feigns sleep and I feign sleep too and soon we are both asleep. In the morning he looks closely at my face.

"Jesus," he says, "you look like you've been plugged in both eyes."

5

Inside, the police station smelled of tomato soup. A ponytailed policewoman stood behind the reception desk beaming.

"Hello and how may I help you today, madam?" she said, and then flushed a bit. I'd parked opposite the police station, thinking I'd sit for a while and figure out what I was going to say, but once I'd put the handbrake on, faces appeared at the window of the station. I tried not to look at them, tried to move in the same way and at the same speed I would have if no one was watching, but I'd forgotten how. My arms felt overly long, and as I crossed the empty road, my bum had more control over my legs than it normally did, and I sashayed stupidly up the steps to the entrance.

I thought about the evidence I had. I would be calm and clear. I reran the day before in my head looking for things to report when I was asked, *Had you noticed anything unusual?*

It had been forecast to snow by the early evening, but my sheep had been unmoved by the news, standing against each other, eyeing me as I moved between them and sprayed their feet for rot. By the time I'd finished, say 3:30, Dog had rolled in goose shit and the wind had picked up, throwing pebbles of water at my face. I walked down the hill into the sea wind, due south. It was cold, a few dead leaves clung to the beech trees. Dog barrelled ahead of me at the perimeter of the woods, black even against the matt darkness of the trees, his ears pricked; he was swallowed by it, sending up a fire of blackbirds, who called loudly and then

31

resettled in other trees, ruffling their feathers and shaking their heads. It would be an early hare, and Dog would have no chance at catching it, would appear back in ten minutes pink-tongued and tired, with a mudded undercarriage.

I looked for strange prints and droppings or hair caught on fences, but all I found was a collection of buzzard pellets. I put my hands in my pockets and felt the grit of them, like compact animals themselves, their leg bones folded into their grey feathery bodies, and my fingers worried them to dust as I walked.

I had stopped at the stile that led onto the bridleway, in the shelter of the hawthorn shrubs that separated the top field from the bottom, and which stretched all the way down to the coastal path. If you stood on the stile you could see the woods in the bottom field, and my cottage, its two storeys looking squat against the slope of the downs. I smoked a cigarette. Down in the bottom field, one of the ewes ate from where the grass was still darkened from the dead sheep. They didn't hold a grudge, sheep.

On the ground at the foot of the stile was a scattering of cigarette butts. Not the kind I smoked—these ones were filterless and the ends had been chewed until they were flat and mulched. I counted seven of them at my feet.

"Bastard kids," I'd said to Dog. I smoked to the end of my cigarette and ground it out on the stile where there was a black mark that the other smoker had made with theirs. I collected the stubs and tucked them all into the empty end of my matchbox. We headed down the bridleway and onto the beach as the sun was starting to go down behind the clouds.

There was a rumble that could have been thunder, and Dog lowered to the ground and then stood up again and looked at me. "It's not my fault," I had told him. He accepted this and carried on fossicking in the razor grass where he usually found something that had dragged itself there to die. There was no way of knowing how long my sheep had lived for, how far she had dragged herself before she died, what she saw.

We'd walked the length of the little bay quickly, and I emptied my pockets of the dust of bones and hair. In the last of the light we went back up the hill with the wind behind us.

The crows roosted in the trees like unopened buds. My stomach growled and I thought of the chicken I'd bought at the weekend. I should stew it, but that would take time; more likely I'd flatten it with a fist and put it in the oven and eat it with bread as soon as it was done.

I rounded the bend of the pathway and stopped dead. A man stood in the shelter of the hedge with his hands in the pockets of his jacket, staring straight ahead. He had a silk scarf wrapped around the bottom half of his face, and wore a suit. His hair was plastered to his head and he had a polythene bag hanging around his wrist. I kept walking as if I hadn't seen him, but clenched my fists until my knuckles clicked. I could smell him, like old vege-tables. We walked home quickly, the thought of the chicken gone. Dog let out a low growl, but kept close to me.

"Fucking kids," I said again, to myself, just to have something to say. I'd tried not to run. I went home and loaded my gun. I looked at the phone and bolted the door.

"I'd like to report a trespasser," I said, and the policewoman busily entered something into her computer. She looked up again.

"Can I have your name please?" She looked me up and down in a way I don't think she expected me to notice. "And, er, your age?"

A policeman came out of a door behind the reception. He had grey hair at his temples and a comfortable-looking jumper on over his regulation one. "I'll take care of this, Gracie," he said, with a swagger. A frown passed over the woman's face.

"Yes, Sarge," she said and tapped more buttons on her keyboard, very quickly.

"This way please." The sergeant opened a perspex gate that said NO ENTRY and ushered me through. The policewoman watched out of the corner of her eye. I felt my bum controlling my legs again.

"Terrible this cold, isn't it?"

I nodded.

"Have to double up on my jerseys." He smiled and plucked at the collar of his jumper. "It's been a busy old month," he said as he showed me down a corridor, "what with Christmas and New Year, and just before that the real-ale festival—literally coach-loads over from the mainland."

Faces looked out from each doorway we passed, people leaning back in their chairs to look up at me.

"Oh," I said.

He opened the door to his office and gave me a small frown and a chuckle. "The problem's more logistics than anything else." He gestured at a chair for me to sit in, and he sat in his behind the desk, and leant back. I noted the window and its view of the edge of Hurst Forest, and the spiny telecom receivers that flagged the prison, hidden deep in the woods. "See, the festival organisers don't provide maps to the place, and I have to send my team out there to direct—to tell the coaches where to park, to answer questions, to direct the whole thing really."

"I see," I said.

"If you ask me, it's the fault of the funders—do not have a festival if you cannot afford the proper and requisite means to staff it." He chopped his hand on the desk firmly and I shifted in my seat. There was a pause.

"I'd like to report a trespasser."

A look came over him. "Now there's an accent we don't hear

34

round these parts much," he said. "I didn't quite hear it before, but it's there, isn't it?"

I smiled and showed my teeth then drew breath to carry on, but he cut in:

"My son-in-law's an Australian," he said, nodding. "They met at a conference in Singapore, would you believe. HR she works in."

I tried to gauge how long a gap was polite to wait before changing the subject back.

"Over in Adelaide now—course the wife's always on that we should go, but my thinking is they can come over here—got a thing about spiders me, you see—know how many different types of spiders you have out there?"

"I—"

"Close to three thousand. Know how many people get bitten each year? Close to four thousand." The policeman sat back in his chair and regarded me. "You do the maths," he said.

"Look." I smiled. Teeth. "It's just that I live alone and—"

"Ah. Lonely place to be, on your own," he said. "Young woman like yourself ought to be with someone. Cheers you right up."

"That's not the problem," I said, trying not to stiffen too much. "It's that someone has been killing my sheep, and now there's some bastard creeping around on my land."

"You a farmer then? Sheep is it? Well, don't hide your light under a bushel, that's a hard job."

"Yes, look, could we . . ." I felt unreasonably hot.

His face took on an entirely different look. "Right," he said. "Let's get a report done, and that way you'll feel better and we can get you back to your sheep, quick smart."

"Great. Thanks."

He took a pen and paper out from a drawer in his desk. "Never could get the hang of computers—I'll throw this over

Gracie's way and she'll type it up no problem. Now, what is your name, pet?"

"What did you call me?"

The air in the room stilled.

"Eh? What's that?" Someone next door coughed. Probably they were listening to us. The sergeant looked at me with mild surprise and a little smile. "I just need your name."

I bit the end of my tongue. "Jake Whyte."

"Address?"

"Coastguard Cottage, Millford."

He looked up, as I knew he would. "Ah, it all makes sense now, doesn't it? You live in old Don Murphy's place."

"Yes. I bought it off him."

"Never see you about. We was all wondering when you'd pop your head out."

I smiled. More teeth.

"Should take yourself out down the pub, make some friends, that'll stop you feeling lonely."

"I'm not lonely."

"Well, if you say so."

"Two of my sheep have been killed."

"Rogue dog you think?"

"No—they've been gutted, sliced about."

"Well, it's amazing what dogs can do—I seen a lurcher go at a fox one time, and just the force *alone* of the dog's snout on the fox's ribs, ripped him right open—no teeth at that point, but fox is a goner. Didn't last much longer after that I can tell you, more or less spat his own stomach out. I don't mind telling you, it was a rough thing to witness."

"Kids have been hanging round the place."

"It's not a great place for kids, the island, I'll give you that—past a certain age anyway. They get bored. Real-ale festival is

36

about all they have to look forward to, and even then they're not supposed to be there." He pointed his biro at me. "Tell you what though, I'll have a word, get them to stop haranguing you."

"How will you know which ones they are?"

The sergeant tapped the side of his nose. "I've a pretty good sense of who's a troublemaker round these parts. Where'd you find them?"

"On the Military Road."

"Military Road? I thought they were trespassing?"

"No, it was someone else, down on the bridleway down to the sea."

"Well, that's not trespassing, is it?"

I fought the urge to knock over his tea, gripped the arms of my chair instead and spoke clearly and slowly:

"It was dark and he shouldn't have been there."

The sergeant narrowed his eyes. "What were you doing there?"

"Going for a walk, but I live there! Look—"

He leant back in his chair. "Listen, Miss Whyte, thing is, no one's done anything."

"My sheep."

"Sheep die all the time—it's like they're trying to get killed, that's what my uncle always said and he should know, had a hundred-acre farm in Wales, blackface lambs, he bred, you never tasted a thing like it."

"I don't think you're taking this seriously," I said and it felt like the limpest thing I'd said in my life.

The sergeant's face went soppy. He spoke softly. "I am taking this seriously, Miss Whyte. I'm taking your happiness and your health seriously. Living alone with all that responsibility? A woman your age? It's not right. You need to get yourself into town once in a while, you need to make friends. Pity the festival's past, because despite my grievances with it, it can be a real laugh." He closed his notebook and smiled broadly at me.

I blinked and closed my mouth. I stood up and tried not to fall over my feet as I walked back up the corridor. The sergeant walked quickly behind me.

"You can always call on us if you just feel a little worried—and if you see the chap again—and he's on your property—let me know."

The policewoman turned to watch me fumble with the catch on the perspex gate, which the sergeant had to help me with. He tried to guide me by touching my elbow, and I jerked away from him.

"Steady," he said, like I'd tripped over.

I thudded down the steps of the station and a light rain spat at my hot face.

"Here's an idea," he called as I climbed into my truck. "Bring some chops or a shoulder for the meat raffle—every Wednesday at the Blacksmith's—that'll win you friends!"

I was vaguely aware of him waving me off but I didn't wave back.

It was early, but I could see a light on in the teahouse, and the owner's car was in the drive. I banged on the door and squinted through my cupped hands against the window to see who was in there. The lady who ran it, who was not all bad, looked up at me and mouthed, *We're closed*, but I stayed there, looking at her. She stared at me a while and seemed to give up, walked towards the door shaking her head. I stepped back to give her room to open the door.

"We're closed—we don't open till eleven o'clock—the bus isn't even running yet."

The bus was a small yellow job that brought tourists from

the smugglers' caves up to the teahouse, which called itself a beauty spot. It looked out over the grey sea, in the other direction so that you couldn't see the mainland. If you got there at the wrong time of day or in the summer, there'd be families and children squawking about, making fusses, telling each other off. When I came I always tried to be the first, so that the place was undisturbed, the tables not sticky, the air not filtered through the open mouths of bored fathers and children's farts.

I didn't move to say anything, just stood there. I needed it. Eventually the woman sighed and opened the door wider to let me in.

"I can't keep doing this you know," she said, and I wiped my boots on the mat before going in. "I'm not even set up—I was just doing the floors. Jacob's not brung in the scones yet, so you'll have to have yesterday's." She didn't wait for a reply, pointed to a table by the window and I sat. "And I haven't laid the tables yet, so you'll just have to wait." I didn't say, *Don't worry about laying a table for me*, because I wanted it laid. With the white paper tablecloth and the ugly doily to go under the plate and under the coffee pot. I wanted the array of cutlery the woman always put out, as though you might eat a scone with a knife, fork and spoon. Three different spoons, one for coffee and one for jam and one for cream. Tongs in the lidded sugar bowl. A white cup for the coffee that had already had hot water in to keep it warm. All of that and the view of the grey sea and nothing beyond it.

The woman was kind even when she was angry. She cleaned away my footprints on her way back to the kitchen, and came out and laid the table while I leant back so she could arrange things. She disappeared and when she came back she'd tied a lacy white apron around her middle, and had maybe put on a touch of lipstick. But she didn't take my order, because she knew already what I wanted. When I'd first arrived on the island, I'd embarrassed myself by asking her for a Devon cream tea.

"I'm afraid an island one will have to do," she had said.

The scone was stale, even though she'd warmed it to try and soften it up. It made no difference. I painted on the cream with one spoon, the jam with another and looked out to sea as I crammed it in my mouth. I didn't like cream but it was okay if you drank strong coffee with it. I warmed my hands around the coffee cup and looked at the empty chair opposite me like it might speak. It didn't.

As we came up the path to the front door, Dog pricked up his ears, and his shoulders thickened. I licked my lips and pictured my gun upstairs, leaning in the cupboard. I tried to open the door quietly, but Dog shot through, his toenails clicking along the stone in the kitchen and up the stairs. I thought I'd left a good thick walking stick by the front door, but it wasn't there any more. There was a stink like something that had been squirted out of an animal. Dog, out of sight, barked and snapped and I pulled a pan off the side and went up after him, holding it high over my head.

From the landing by my bedroom came a bang. The banisters shook as I pounded up the stairs. On the landing Dog danced around a large pigeon, its wing bent at an angle that was wrong, a string of blood over its back.

"Dog!" I shouted and he looked at me, the fury gone, his tail wagging and a feather hanging off his lip. I dropped my arms and breathed out, leant for a moment on the banister. Dog's tongue lolled out and I caught hold of the fur at the back of his neck before he went for it again.

"Okay, bird," I said. "Okay." And it looked at me. I could see its heart moving in its chest, and all there was to do was to go

40

towards it and pick it up. It let me get at it around the middle, carefully avoiding the mashed wing. Its heart buzzed but it was still in my hands. Dog whined.

"Dog," I said, "no." And he sat down, then stood up again.

One of the pigeon's legs bicycled out, and there was a ring around the foot. I held the bird to my chest with one hand and unravelled the ring with the other. Just a phone number, which was good—I wouldn't have to make the decision about whether or not to wring its neck.

"Get me the phone," I told Dog.

We all three went to the phone together and I dialled the number.

The man who picked up didn't say hello, he said, "Esler."

"I have a pigeon with your phone number on," I said.

The man was silent.

"He's hurt his wing."

"Is it dead?" he said.

"No, just hurt. The wing."

The man sighed. "Pop her in a shoebox, keep her warm and watered. If she makes it through the night she'll tell you when she's well enough to fly home."

He hung up.

"Dickhead," I said to the pigeon. Any shoes I bought came in a plastic bag. I took another look at the bird, saw that its bottom eyelid had closed and its head was slack on its neck, and that talking to the man on the phone, I'd squeezed it too hard and now it was dead.

I took the pigeon, wrapped in newspaper like a fish supper, down to the shore. Dog pranced next to me with a light in his eyes that meant killing, and I tried to keep the atmosphere mellow and not like the disposal of a tame bird that I'd murdered. It was not a beautiful beach for a burial at sea. A skin of seaweed had washed up on the rocks and jumped with sea lice. Black rocks rose all around it so that if you didn't know your path back up, you could feel trapped. There was no accounting for the places the English took their children—in the early days I came across a young family in mud up to their thighs, crashing around by the hawthorn stile, lost in the dark with a toddler swaddled onto each of their backs. The woman with tear-streaks down her face and the man white and grateful for the lift back to their bed and breakfast. "Not a good place to get lost," I'd enjoyed telling them on the drive; "you were just a few yards from a pretty sheer cliff-face." Which was half true.

My first summer on the island, I'd cooked my tea on the beach, drunk beer wrapped in a blanket, listening to the waves break, watching the lights come on over on the mainland, while my eyes got used to the black sea with the moon tripping off it at the horizon. I had it in my head to do it the next summer, but the breaks between rain got smaller and sometimes there was a smell on the beach around dusk, something between burnt rubber and silage.

Dog ate a dead crab. I heard it being broken apart, turning to dust. A drizzle started and gave a silver fringe to his fur. He finished his crab and saw something in the dry grasses on the bank and pricked his ears. He moved up the slope, his legs bent at the knees, and disappeared over a dune, the back-kick of his leg picking up speed. While he was occupied, and so that he wouldn't chase the bird out into the water and crunch her up too, I waded out a little way in my gumboots, which, it turned out, had a hole in each of them small enough to be invisible to the naked eye but large enough to let in frozen water, which chafed at my heels and then crept up my socks. I rolled the bird out of the newspaper and let her float into the sea. She tried to

come back in a few times, but eventually after some encourage-
ment she floated past the small breakers, her chest white and dry
and her broken wing pointing upwards as she went further and
further out and then sank, like the sea had swallowed her. I
hummed the song from *Titanic*.

6

Outside Kambalda is a shearers' pub which isn't much more than a galvanised shed with a bar and tables made out of railway sleepers. They serve whisky in mugs and everything else is canned. You're supposed to bring your own cooler, and I make a mental note to pick one up next time we see a shop, which could be weeks from now. I'm at the bar, turning a mug of whisky in my hands and taking longer than I should because a feeling's come over me like I'm on the outside of myself, and how did I end up at this bar in the middle of a desert with the smell of a barbecue coming in through the open wall of the shed, and with all these men, not another woman in running distance, and how is it that this is a strange comfort, and how long will it last before something finds me again and I have to go somewhere else. One of the younger blokes, Connor, comes and slouches next to me.

"You right?" he says.

I nod.

He inspects the dirt underneath his fingernails, decides it's right just the way it is and starts to roll a smoke. "Fitting in pretty good, for a chick." I look up. He points to his tobacco with his eyebrows raised.

"Ta," I say and he takes out another paper to roll me one too. I have a friend.

"So where were you before here?" he asks, and a ripple goes through me.

"I worked for my uncle on a station up north." I hate myself for the lie, not because it's a lie but because it's a stupid one and I should have been prepared.

"Your uncle has a station? Where north?"

Don't think about it or he'll know you've made it up.

"Marble Bar."

"Marble Bar? I know Marble Bar—maybe I've worked his station, what's his name?"

I can feel now the sweat is beading on my upper lip and forehead. I fight to control the flush of my face.

"He's dead," I say. "He died, it was really bad."

Connor grimaces. "Jeeze, sorry to hear it," he says, looking uncomfortable, but he opens his mouth and I know he still wants the name of the uncle, and so I cut in and a story comes out that has nothing to do with my brain.

"He was trampled." Again Connor looks like he wants to ask a question, so I cut him off. "Sheep got spooked by a storm—went crazy." I am sure Connor's never heard of a death by sheep-trampling; there's a look on his face for a moment when he seems like he might think I'm joking with him and so to stop him, I say, "The head came clean off."

Whether or not Connor believes me, his eyes are wide, and he has stopped trying to ask questions. Perhaps he thinks I am a mental case, which is fine. He raises his drink. "Fuck me," he says. "Well, jeeze—these things are liable to happen to a bloke working out in these sorts of places. Sheep can be flighty bastards—got no loyalty, not like dogs." He hands me a roll-up and lights mine first then his. He clinks my mug softly with his can. "To Uncle . . ." He leaves a gap for me to fill the name.

"John." I say Dad's name, a name that always seemed too fancy and European for him.

"To Uncle John." And we drain our drinks and go and sit back at the table.

Clare is beasting the kid, calling him nicknames that don't mean anything much but which make Bean go red in his pale cheeks, as if his real name wasn't bad enough. *Nippy Balls, Sour Tit, Pussy Willow.* He won't leave the kid alone, but it is pretty funny.

"G'wan, Ball Ache," says Clare, "show us where your dick's hidden." Clare pulls a stool up opposite me and gestures for Bean to sit. "Let's see who wins a wrestle between you and Alice the Goon here." Mostly the men laugh, but not all of them. There's a quiet moment when Bean and I look at each other. I would like for this not to happen, and when Bean sits opposite me with a look of drunken determination coming over him, it breezes through me that if I let him win, then maybe he'll get less of a hard time. But I won't do that, I know it as I settle my elbow on the table. Bean will have to fend for himself; he might be small and awkward, but I am a woman on a sheep station. We grip hands over the sleepers, position our elbows to everyone's satisfaction, and money starts getting laid down. I catch Greg's eye and he smiles at me, holds up twenty dollars. I see Bean's white biceps bulge like a new potato, and there's a countdown shouted by everyone. The kid's face goes red and fierce, his lips pull back from his teeth, and it's not a total pushover. There's some strength in him, but mainly it's the strength of fear, like those times you hear about kids lifting lorries off their parents. Our fists wobble in the centre, but soon Bean has used up his burst of self-belief, and his face sweats and he is tired and done. I start to push his arm down, and I see in his face the huge disappointment, he had thought this was his time to be hoicked onto the shoulders of the men, for his movie-self to be stronger than he looked, but once we are

46

three-quarters of the way down, he has no way back up and I flatten him and everyone cheers and whoops, and Bean lays his head on his spent arm.

Later, when I am drunk, and Bean has been relegated back at the end of the table, where Denis now and again asks him a question and then doesn't listen to the answer, Greg sits himself in front of me and puts up his massive arm. I laugh and he laughs and I put my arm up too, like we're about to wrestle, but all we do is grip hands like that.

"Strong lady," he says.

In the morning, I wake up in between Greg's bear arms. I hold my breath and count to fifty. Okay, I say to myself, okay, and I check through my body from the feet up. All is warm and nothing hurts except the crick in my neck from lying on his shoulder. The smell of him, lanolin and whisky that has been sweated out of him in the night.

The sun is rising and there won't be long before the gong goes and work starts, and with the hangover worming in my guts I try to roll softly from the bed. In a sitting position, I'm about to make it, when Greg springs from where he is lying and makes a noise like a lion, grabs me by the waist and wrestles me back into the bed, growling and grunting into my neck and squeezing me hard. It takes me a few seconds to understand that this is a joke and I laugh.

Just like the other times it has happened, the rest of the day we will catch little looks at each other and I will worry and feel good and feel sick and trip up over my feet. It is simple in a way I thought wasn't possible. At smoko he will sit opposite me on the bench and touch my knee under the table, and when I look up at him he will wink. It's getting so when he touches me I don't even think about pushing his hand away and I will even give myself a shock by walking past him while he's bent over a bucket washing his hands, and thwacking him on the behind before I can stop myself. He will jump up and crack a smile that cuts his face up into segments—it's a face I like, it's wide and has a tendency to smile.

Clare is missing from tea and I see him over at the phone-stand behind the shed. He's nodding and he's looking at me in a way that I don't like. He turns his back, and finishes up the call. I drink deeply and feel better. It's just the paranoia, and maybe I could lighten up on the drinking.

"Who's that?" asks Greg when Clare comes back to the table. He doesn't often use the phone, none of us do, other than poor Bean who misses his sixteen-year-old girlfriend in Rock-hampton.

Clare looks up brightly. "Just Ben—letting us know what a dickhead he is. Reckons he likes the uni course, reckons next time we see him he'll be air-conditioned and rich."

"Ha!" says Greg.

"Prick," says Connor.

Clare looks at me and smiles. I shift in my seat.

Bean sits apart from everyone else. Greg strides past and clunks a beer down in front of him without speaking, and the boy's face opens and he looks happy as he sits there chewing his meat and drinking his beer.

Later, Clare is in a bad mood with the drink, and even Denis seems to enjoy winding him up.

"Gettin' a bit soft around the middle," Denis says, prodding Clare's gut with a bony finger. "Finding it slows you down in the shed?"

"Get fucked, you old cunt," says Clare, but it only makes Denis chuckle and his eyes shine. Denis is too old to say much to, and so Clare rounds on me. "Y'know," he says, "they won't have a woman at sea—reckon it's bad luck. They reckon a clothed woman on board is bad luck, angers the seas." I square myself up and look directly at him, but he doesn't want to meet my eyes. I know I look hench, but I can feel a nasty beat to my heart.

He knocks back the rest of his drink. "It's just not right, it's just not!" he belts out. "In me old man's day, there's no way they would have tolerated it."

"I dunno," says Greg, "your old man gave you a girl's name. Reckon he might have been quite progressive." Everyone laughs a bit.

Clare is red in the face and Greg smiles behind his drink. Clare stands up abruptly and sways over the bench.

"You'se are all fuckin' poofs," he says and flounces away into the night.

With Greg breathing like a tanker next to me, I draw up a contract in my head with Dad. This will not go on for long, I will keep moving. In return he will sink beneath these new memories, just for a while. He only exists now as the money in my bank account. I can keep it all at arm's length because there is nothing here yet to connect me to that time, with those people, other than the marks on my back which are pinked over enough to look like they happened in a past that can be left alone.

In the morning Greg traces the scars with his fingers. "Those are hell good," he says with real admiration in his voice. "How'd you get 'em?"

I turn and look at him and feel that countdown, how it could go either way. "Bad relationship."

Greg shifts up the bed and puts his hand on the back of my neck, like there's something I deserve comfort for. I can let myself believe it just for now that I am some kind of victim. He lifts my hair up and I can feel him looking. He kisses the top bone of my spine and says, "I'll kill him." And there it is, the lie, and it becomes real, another contract signed, stamped and dated.

There's a yell, which turns into a scream. Greg shoots out of bed in his undies and runs towards the noise. By the time I make it over to the shed, everyone's standing in a circle around the grinder. Blood is misted up the wall and Bean is on the floor sobbing and holding what is left of his hand. Greg is trying to get him to hold it up above his heart, but the kid won't have it, can't stop looking at it.

Someone's gone to call the Flying Doctors and Alan comes running out of the house, his face white and red at the same time. He pushes men out of the way and squats down on the other side of Bean, inspects the hand and holds out his palm to Connor. "Gimmie yer bloody singlet," he says, quietly, and Connor strips it off.

"Okay, Arthur," says Alan to Bean, "bloody doctors are on their way." He tears the singlet in two down the middle and ties it with a firmness that makes me wince around the kid's wrist. "There's nothing here can't be sorted out," he says and Bean carries on sobbing. There's no getting to him.

"What the fuck was he doing on the bloody grinder?" Alan hisses at us. Clare is standing at the back with a hand over his face. He raises his arm.

"He was sharpening my gear for me." There's a silence, deeper than before, and everyone turns to look at Clare. Alan's mouth drops open, but he doesn't say anything. Clare walks a little way away from us.

"We'll get yer mum on the bloody phone," says Alan to Bean. "She'll be there by the time they've got you sorted out."

When the plane lands, they're worried about the blood loss, and Alan goes with them to the hospital. Bean is blue in the lips as he's carried, between Alan and the medic, into the plane. Clare kicks over and over again at a stump of wood stuck in the earth.

We get on with work, I go back to roustabout without being asked, just seems the right thing. Clare is slow and hardly makes his quota. No one talks. The next morning, Alan is back and you can hear him going off at Clare round the back of the sleeping shed.

"What the fuck were you thinking? The bloody hand's gone, mate. Kid can't read. Certainly can't fucking write now. What the bloody fuck do you think he's going to do for a job? That's it, you've fucking fucked it. I had to tell his mother—fuck, I told her I'd bloody look after him." It goes on, and every question Alan asks is left unanswered by Clare. Everyone pretends not to have heard any of it, and Clare comes limping pale into the shed, to start work. Most of the men make an effort to turn their backs to him, Denis mutters something under his breath. But Greg slaps him on the shoulder and says, "You right?" Clare nods and takes up his position. I hand him a sheep and it's all go but we work in silence.

Just after midday Alan comes in and when he sees me flinging a fleece onto the table he goes apeshit. "Why in filthy bloody fuck are you doing that?" I stiffen and feel my eyes stretching wide. But the shouting's not for me. He turns to Clare and points at him. "You, you useless fuck, until further notice, you're bloody roustabout, not Jake." Clare's mouth is open. "I'm not losing a prime shearer just because you can't look after your own shit." I don't know where to look or what to do. No one moves. "Jake, where's your bloody kit?"

"Back in my room."

"Go and get it, you're on." I take a second to respond. "G'wan, get!" he barks, and I scuttle off across the yard to my room. It's awful; it's humiliating for Clare, poor Bean's life is wrecked, Alan is all kinds of fucked-up, but I can't stop smiling.

7

I watched out the kitchen window as the sun melted behind the wood. The fading white shapes of sheep on the black grass. When the air turned thick and dark I drew the curtains above the sink and turned on all the lights.

A sheep coughed loudly from the bottom paddock and Dog pricked up his ears. Stew sweated in its pan on the Rayburn. The radio played out the soccer report and I spread the table with newspaper so I could pick apart my shears, sharpen the teeth and oil and polish them. I took my time, put a pot of coffee on the stove, stirred the stew. I sharpened every tooth until they were perfect. I finished my coffee and poured whisky, restrung my shears, and then wondered what would happen if I tried to shear the dog.

I cut fat slabs of white bread and left a black thumbprint in the butter. I spooned stew into a bowl and poured another whisky to go with it. I poured some into the stew as well. The cough came again and I remembered that I'd moved them all to the top paddock away from the woods. I cracked my mug down on the counter and Dog let out a small growl. I went upstairs for the gun and tried not to think about why I was getting it. There was not supposed to be much you could do with a gun in England you couldn't do with a rock, but I was less sure of that now.

The night had settled in, but a full moon lit up the paddock, slid over the backs of the sheep in the top field. Dog let out another deep growl—and the cough echoed from inside the woolshed, not the field. I stayed still. The sheep were motionless on the hillside. A field of ghosts.

Dog was snuffing at the shed door and barked. The cough again, this time followed by a moan. Blood pumped in my fists. *Just a wounded fox*, I thought, *just the wind rattling through a fracture in the grate, just a ringing in my ears.*

The shed door was a crack open and inside the darkness coddled like black water. Dog disappeared into it and I cocked the gun and went for the switch. The light blinked on, ticking, flashing green and then yellow, and I watched in slices as in the corner Dog attacked something large, hacking and snarling. I was stuck for a moment with my mouth open, then I trained my gun.

"Jesus!" screamed a man's voice. Dog had hold of his wrist, shook it hard.

"Who the fuck are you?" I shouted and whether I meant it or not, my gun went off. Dog fell to the floor, and for a terrible second I thought I'd shot him, but he was just gun-shy. The man covered his face with his hands and didn't move. My arms shook, and I lowered the gun. No one was dead, and the man didn't appear shot. I had to put the gun down before I dropped it.

"What do you want? Did you kill my sheep? Who sent you?" I barked. The man didn't answer, just sat there, covering his face.

Dog sloped back to stand next to me, his fight gone.

"What do you want?" I said again loudly. I thought about getting the gun again but my arms had lost their strength, I felt them flapping at my sides.

"I want to sleep," said the man. "I only want to sleep." His voice was thick and swollen, just a croak. He lowered his hands. It was the man from the hedgerow. "You didn't have to shoot at me," he said and met my eyes. "God," he said, "you look awful. Do you cut your own hair?"

I took a step forward to look at him in the green light. A wet sleeping bag draped around his shoulders.

"Why are you here?" I asked again in my most menacing voice. I could smell the drink on him. His beard had crept up to the very tops of his cheeks. His exposed hand had a number of punctures in it, from Dog. I swallowed. "What do you want from me?"

"I just wanted to sleep in your shed—" The end of his sentence collapsed into a coughing fit.

I cleared my throat. "Is it you? Have you been killing my sheep? Have you been in my house? Have you been banging around in my house at night?"

He looked at me with eyes pink from coughing. His jaw shuddered from the cold. "I don't understand you," he said.

There was a fleck of blood on his lower lip, from where he must've bit himself.

He looked at me, one of his eyes drooped a little. "I did not kill a sheep."

He was having trouble keeping his eyes open. My heart pumped thickly.

"I didn't shoot you, did I?"

He opened his eyes again. "What on earth are you on about now?" he said, exasperated, like I was bothering him with some kind of ridiculous information. Rain had started up and it drummed on the roof. I didn't know how I could move him.

"I'll call the police if you don't leave right now," I said. The man made no response. I watched him for some time. He didn't move, just his chest rising and falling, just the moustache hairs blowing in his breath. I nudged him hard in the leg with the toe of my boot.

"You can stay here the night," I said. He opened his eyes wide again. "But in the morning, you have to leave."

"Thank you."

"If you don't leave in the morning, I will shoot you," I said, but his eyes had closed and he was already asleep.

He was sitting on the bare concrete, wrapped sadly in his wet sleeping bag. I left him there, turning off the light as I went and taking my gun.

It could have been the air, the wind. It could have been that out there in the dark, all of my sheep had turned to stare at me. Or that something pulled itself out of the sea and lumbered up the path towards me. But it wasn't. It was only the night like I'd seen it a thousand times before, alone.

Inside, I looked at the telephone, imagined the sergeant's face and then turned away from it again. I thought of how Don'd tell me to call on those young farmers.

In the kitchen I looked at the bread I'd cut. I put the coffee back on the stove and sat down. I got up and went to the boiler cupboard and found a scratchy blanket and took it back out to the shed. I could hear his breath wheezing in and out of him at the doorway, and I didn't need the light on to know where he was and that he was still sleeping. I cleared my throat a few times, but he didn't wake and so I laid the blanket over him then walked back to the house, trying to go without urgency. I bolted the door and checked the windows.

I poured whisky into my coffee and took it upstairs to bed. Dog came with me. I sat on the edge of the bed a while and then went back downstairs with Dog. I pointed at the front door. "Stay," I said, and Dog raised his eyebrows, but lay down with his chin on his paws.

I took the bottle of whisky up with me, and half an hour later came back down the stairs and found Dog curled on the sofa. I rang home and no one answered, everyone was out, living their lives in the way that they did. If the phone was in the same place in the hallway, resting on its same wicker cabinet, it faced out towards the front garden, unkempt, fireweed and dead leaves, brown snakes and bindi-eye. Butcher birds caught mice in those places, speared them on the branches of the jacaranda, dead mice and voles. I hung up. I collected all the knives I could find into a roasting tin, and on second thought the carving fork too, and took them up to bed with me. I turned off the light and pulled a stool to the window and propped the gun up next to it. I sat and waited for my eyes to get used to the dark and I watched the door of the shed with a mug of whisky in my hand.

8

By the time I reach Kalgoorlie, something is rattling badly under the bonnet of the truck. The kangaroo seems a long time ago, but it did more damage than I'd first thought. There are no papers in the glove compartment, only WD-40, an open bag of peanuts and an empty pack of condoms. The best I can do for her is to sell her to a scrapyard. I cut the engine in the wreckers' yard and count the ticks for the last time. When they stop, I know I've arrived somewhere else.

Along the journey the roll of money from Otto's tin became thin, and there have been moments when, sat in the truck in the dark, I've thought about going back to the old way. But that person is like someone I've never known. The thought of it—of the flesh and the smell and noise of it, the ache and hollow afterwards, the taste that makes drink curdle and turn thick in your throat—it makes me clench my fists so that my nails dig into my palms. I have had dreams sleeping in the locked cab of the truck of gritting my teeth until they break, until they shatter inside my mouth, and when I wake up I expect to see his face at the window, looking in at me. Some nights I've woken up and I can hear someone singing, *Is it you or is it me? Lately I've been lost it seems* . . . and then it turns out just to be the drill of a nightjar, or a fruit bat complaining in its tree. While the sun comes up I stare at myself in the rear-view mirror, holding my own gaze until I am just a blur, like when you say your own name over and over until it doesn't make sense any more.

I get only $45 for the truck, but there is something good about thinking of it taken apart, limb from limb, the licence plate nailed up on a wall, just one among hundreds, unseen and ignored, the last link to him disintegrated and untraceable. I spend the last of the money on a sleeping bag, a change of clothes and a backpack to put it all in.

"Those are big bloody bastards," says a man called Alan, holding my palms open on the bar of the Fleeced Lamb in Kalgoorlie. There's something in the businesslike way he holds my hands which makes me relax—like he's looking at the hoof of a goat. "You'll be right, love," he says. "Look like you can bloody look after yourself, I bloody reckon." He lets go of my hands, and drains his drink before fixing me with his eyes again. "Reckon you're the sort with an old soul, and that's just the sort I like."

Alan is the bloke I've tracked down who has advertised for a new roustabout. It's the only sheep job that doesn't say, "Skill Level: Experienced" next to it; instead it says "Skill Level: Intermediate," but Alan's interview is pretty much: "You scared of bloody sheep at all?" and when I say no and he has a look at my arms, it seems a done deal, and he doesn't even glance at the side-of-paper CV I printed off in the Internet café which is made up.

When the first day in Alan's team comes, it has me feeling sick, like there's a test I don't know how to pass, but no one looks surprised to see a woman in the woolshed where the tin roof keeps the heat in, and pushes it down on our heads. It smells like piss and burnt hair, but I've smelled worse things.

"I'm Jake," I say to the men. I hold up my hand, and they look back, six of them all the same, the same hats and jeans, the same sun-dark skin and hair that pokes out just a little bit at the sides.

Someone says, "G'day mate," and two of them lift their hands back at me. One of them pushes his hat to the back of his head to look at me and smiles. He's got a wide face, deep-set blue eyes.

"You the cook, mate?" asks a man with a red moustache and someone answers for me, telling me, "Nah, Sid's cook. Sid Hargreve." And I breathe out, thinking of feeding all those men burnt chops and eggs.

"She's bloody roustabout for now," Alan says from behind me, "an' we'll see how she goes from there." He claps me on the back. "She's got a pair of shoulders on her," and there's a nod from most of the men—they have seen stranger things—and they all turn back to their gear, checking blades and blowing dust and sheep skin out from behind the teeth. At the side of the shed I can hear a mechanical grinder at work. One of the men stands still, holding his shears and just looking, with no expression I can understand. A sweat breaks out on my upper lip. I'd like a smoke, but not in front of everyone.

Alan shows me where I'll sleep.

"We get a woman now and again working with us—no one that's stayed on too long. I'm not bloody prejudice," he says, "but sleeping is the tricky bloody thing. If I get caught not offering you a separate room, I'm in the bloody poo." He shows me into the shed where there are two utes parked and a dirt bike. There's a cot-bed set up in a corner of the shed, which is a work area—the bench has been cleared of tools and petrol and given a wipe down. There's a green plastic washing-up basin there and a bar of soap. "Also, I'm supposed to provide a separate bloody washing facility. There's a tap round the back."

He turns and looks me up and down. "How are ya with spiders?"

*   *   *

Ben is the roustabout I'll be taking over from and for the first two days, he shows me the ropes. "It's a hard job," he says, and he eyes my shoulders, "but I reckon you'd do all right." He grabs a ewe by the front legs, flips her over and drags her backwards towards one of the men who is on his final strokes. As he picks up the finished fleece, a swarm of blue bottles tumbles off it, more crawl than fly. Ben shows me how to fling it onto the table. I try and look like it's harder than it is.

"What'll you do next?" I ask.

"Going to uni to do agriculture, they've got a course at the Hedland I've got a place on," he says. My jaw sets at the mention of the Hedland. One of the men overhears our conversation.

"Little fucker's got ideas—reckons we'll be working for him in a few years."

Everyone laughs as if this is the most tragic delusion a person could be under.

Ben rolls his eyes and gives the man the finger. The man smiles and goes back to his sheep. "Part of the job," he says, hoicking another sheep up by the legs, "is copping shit from this lot."

I'm good at the job, I can feel it, better already maybe than Ben is, but I don't want him to dislike me, so I hold back, let him bark at me a few times so that it's understood that I'm the new one, the arsehole without a clue. The sheep are thicker than the ones at Otto's and they have more fight in them, but we get along fine. It's good to feel the fat on their bones, the grease from their wool on my palms, like they've got it to spare. I learn the names of the men as we go along, listening in on conversations, and the stuff they shout at each other over the buzz of the clippers. There's the tall one with a heavy-looking skull, who seems quiet until one of the others starts to tell a joke. I miss the first part because I'm watching the way the one telling the joke breezes through the wool, right at the root. He takes ages with

61

his joke, because he has to breathe in that way with the sheep round him, and when the fleece falls to the ground and I take him a new sheep, he shaves her soft underbelly and stops telling his joke, and I hold my breath with him, as he palpates her around the groin, getting the skin there taut. On the joke goes, something with monkeys and cannons and dicks. When he's finished with the sheep he straightens up and says the punchline: "And she says, 'That's just what my husband said, Reverend.'"

The tall one is working on the long blow of a ewe and he hugs her to him while he's laughing, holding the shears away from her, and he says, "Shit, Clare, you're an arsehole." And he gives his sheep a pat on the head like she is in on the joke too, before carrying on with the shear; a chuckle comes now and again from him, small shakes of his head. His name is Greg.

Sid the cook feeds us stew with some bread he's baked. The bread is like wet cement inside and it sticks to the bottom of my stomach and sets. The stew is brown mutton. I can't take the taste of it, which coats my tongue and smells of death.

"Watchin' yer weight?" asks the one called Clare when he looks at my plate, and so I smile and shovel a forkful in just to show it doesn't bother me. My stomach contracts and sweat pricks out on the back of my neck. I smile wider.

No one complains or compliments Sid, who doesn't seem to expect it. We get the same for tea, but with a steamed jam and sponge pudding out of tins, and Alan sets up a bar. You write down the drinks you take in a ledger and it comes out of your wages. I take a six pack and offer one to Ben as a friendly thing. Ben is pleased, says he's spent most of his wages buying drinks he owes the shearers.

"Fuckin' bastards, had me today," he says, but he says it smiling and someone walks past and tweaks his tit.

* * *

62

In the shed there's no door to close, and so I can see the night sky from where I lie. I get up and root around in a drawer until I find a hammer, and then I put it under my bed, just as a comforter. The sky is big and thrown with stars. The shed smells of diesel, which is not a bad smell, and once I spot the huntsmen up on the ceiling like fat grey stars themselves, I'm happy as long as they're still. I fall asleep and dream nothing, nothing touches me in the dark.

In the morning I wash at my basin on the workbench, with an old singlet for a sponge. There are kookaburras and miner birds racketing about, and I wonder that I never heard them at Otto's, just the morning buzz of blowflies.

Once the sheep have been mustered and are secured in their runs, my job is to keep the pens full and to get the sheep to the shearers so they don't have more than a couple of breaths before starting on the next one. Then I fling the fleeces up on the wool table, where an old bloke called Denis skirts them and all the dags and maggoty bits fall through the slats in the table, because people don't want shit in their jumpers, or even in their carpets. I can see a couple of the men hang back a little, and expect me to take my time, to be slow. There's that solid heat that gets bounced down on us from the tin roof, and the flies in here are fat and damp—when they land around your mouth you feel like you've been kissed by something dead.

Clare calls out, "Hope you know the tradition, girlie—if there's fleece on the boards and no sheep in my arms, you owe me a beer." I ignore him, because I can already tell he is the one to ignore.

Everyone takes their places, I have a sheep to each man, and I wait to see how quickly they go. There are two, Connor and Stuart, who work side by side and they are the quickest, because they make it into a race. At the start of work they give themselves a countdown, "Three, two, one, go!" and they are off, as fast as they can. There are a few nicks on Connor's sheep, and they wobble back into the out-run looking a bit scrubby. Greg's sheep are sleek and clean with no grazes, like they've been buttered, and so are Clare's. They're fast too, but only Clare is competitive. Greg won't be drawn into a race, just smiles, but Clare races him anyway.

The day's work is drawing to a close and Greg asks if I've ever tried to shear a sheep before. He smiles in that way that's started to make my tongue do roll-ups in my closed mouth. "Reckon you'd be good at it."

"Couple a times," I say.

"Have a go of this one, long as you don't cut her in half," he says, and he catches his sheep under the front legs, and holds it for me with a nod towards the back strap. "Put that on, helps take the weight." I pause and look at the strap.

"I'm fine without it." I'm worried it will change the weight and feel of the sheep, make it less natural. My back still feels knotted together and strong.

Greg raises his eyebrows. "Whatever madam prefers." But he clearly doesn't think I can manage it. "I can hold her for you if you like," he says, and I let him lock around me with his arms. The contact makes my mouth go dry but I concentrate on hiding that, and it feels different. He smells like sawdust.

His shears are sharper and fancier than the ones Otto had, and it takes me a moment to understand them. I take off the belly wool first, and the new shears are so simple, they hardly stick at all. It's so easy and I can feel the sheep relaxing under Greg's arm, and when I start at her neck, I get it all, and I get it well, and quickly with just about the minimum amount of strokes. Once her fleece is lying on the floor, intact and full, and she has wobbled away with no trace of red on her, I wipe the sweat off

64

my upper lip and Greg steps away from me with his hands on his hips. "Well, shit, where'd you learn that?" and behind him, Stuart and Connor who have come to watch start laughing. Clare walks out of the shed.

It's too hot, but I like the way the heat makes my arms feel like they're full of warm oil, and sweat runs down them in sheets soaking the sides of my singlet. There's an ache in the bottom of my spine from bending and lifting, but it beats lying on my bed at Otto's waiting for the day to be over. I catch myself smiling as I throw another fleece onto the table and Denis nods to me, impressed. I don't pull the sheep as strongly as Ben did, I wrap part of my arm around their middle, so their legs don't drag, and in return they don't buck as much, and it goes smoothly. No one comments on it, so I reckon it's not a bad thing. At the end of the day, my arms bulge at my shirtsleeves and I'm on the nose, but so is everyone else, and when I go for a proper wash behind my sleeping quarters where there's a small pallet shower with an open top, my body feels like a new one; I can picture the layers coming away, the dirt and the grot and old terrible skin. I'm pulling a singlet on over my head when I hear someone cough, and I snap around, my heart barrelling about inside me; my eyes dart to the hammer underneath the bed. It's Connor, looking embarrassed.

"Sorry, mate," he says, "forgot you were in here—just come to get some oil for the grinder." I smile hard while he locates the oil and nods to me as he leaves. I try not to think about what he might be thinking if he saw my back. It's dark in the shed, and probably he didn't see a thing. I breathe and close my eyes for a few moments before setting off to find the others. They're sat at a long table out in the field; Connor is there and looks normal. I take a place at the end of the table and try to relax. Greg sits

himself next to me and hands me a beer. Panic is replaced by a
warm feeling.

A skinny boy everyone calls Bean who is younger than me and
has a voice that is perfect for copying comes along. Clare
says Bean sounds like a donkey getting its dick yanked, and when
Bean blushes I stand with everyone else and smile. Bean is there
to bloody replace me, Alan says, and for a moment I think I'm
being fired, but he's telling me to get in with the shearers.

Clare is shitful to Bean, who struggles to tow a sheep out of
the pen. Bean screams and goes bright red when one of them
bites him. *Poor sod*, I think, and I show him how to grab them
so they don't freak out. *Why'd you have to have such a crap name*,
I think, *you could have got away with the rest of it.*

I love being in the line and working the day out. I notice Clare
watching and I feel him racing me. I try not to be bothered by
it, but he cuts a sheep badly, and he shouts, "Fuckit!" and chews
Bean out like it's his fault. "Get me the tar, you fucking retard!"
he shouts.

"Calm down, man," says Greg, and Clare shrugs, ignoring him.
I catch Bean's eye and smile, and he turns away. He probably only
just got away from his mum, doesn't want to team up with the
only woman.

We're not that far from a small town with a pub and a bank
and a supermarket, and on my half day, I go to the bank so I can
see about getting my wages to go straight in. It's been a long
time since I've used a bank. The cashier has a small frown when
she looks at my statement, but I ignore it, not offering an explan-
ation. She turns the screen so I can see it. Three months ago, my
mother deposited fifty thousand dollars into my account. I stare
at the screen, and mutely hand over my payroll details.

It takes me three goes to ring home. The first time I dial the number and hang up immediately. Then I let it ring once. The next time, Iris is quick and answers on the first ring.

"Oh," she says, "it's you."

I struggle to get my voice out. "Hi, Iris. How are you?"

She snorts. "Never mind that. You get the money? I didn't think Mum should've given it to you, but we didn't know how else to get a response."

"What's the money from?"

"Dad's dead. An accident at the marina."

The last time I saw Dad, his face tight with anger, and then a time before when just the two of us went surfing, when I was ten. He had salt in the sun-creases of his eyes. My mouth struggles to open.

"When?"

"Nine months ago. Give or take."

I am dipped in silence. "I can't believe it" is all I can say.

She snorts again. "Yeah, well. I can't believe a lot of things that go on."

The silence is broken by the pips on the phone and I put in two more dollars. The news has not hit my body yet, or my brain.

"How's Mum?"

"She's batshit."

"Is she there?"

"No." But Iris keeps her voice low and quiet.

"The triplets?"

"They're meatheads. Look, I've got stuff to be doing."

"Will you tell her I rang?"

"Sure," says Iris, and I know, I remember the tone that means she won't. "Just what she needs is a good long chat with you. You've always been so supportive."

Iris hangs up without asking how to contact me. I don't even

67

know how Dad died. *An accident at the marina?* Was he still at the packing yard? Was he drunk?

On the drive back to the station, Dad feels like an orange in my sternum. I repeat the words over and over in my head, *Dad's died, Dad's died,* until they don't mean anything. None of it means anything if I ignore it; my father was alive until I went to the bank and saw the money there. I won't tell anyone about the money, or that my father is dead. I won't touch the money unless I have to.

9

I woke curled around the stool, with a headache. Dog was in the bed, under the covers.

The shed was empty. The blanket was folded neatly and hung from the teeth of the rake. Up on the paddock crows dive-bombed something, seagulls formed lazy circles above them. There was spit in the air, but dark brown clouds hanging low promised something more impressive was on its way. Here and there on the slope of the field were old tree trunks whose roots had been too deep to pull out when the land was cleared, long, long ago. Some were split and hollowed out, eaten by wasps, and grew a fungi that Don called Jew's ears. Those trunks sitting there, with the wars starting and finishing around them, horses being overtaken by tractors, the birth of Don, probably the birth of his father, certainly his father's death. It made me feel lonely to think about it, that old English history in the dark and the wet, the short days with no electricity. It made me want to go and sit in the truck, rev the throttle, just to remind myself of my century, just to feel the modern dry heat of the engine. My feet squeaked inside my boots, wet already. I lit a cigarette to dry the air around me. Sheep followed behind, with lazy questions about feeding time. At the top of the hill, I watched a merlin sweep the edge of the woods, like she couldn't find a way in, like no tree was quite the right tree to settle on. She let out a screech and was suddenly gone. A burst of small birds jumped out of the treetops and then sank back in. The trees appeared to swell and shrink with the rhythm of breath.

Over the other side of the hill, I found a pregnant ewe stuck in the drainage. Her muzzle was black with mud, like she'd been trying to lift herself free with her face. I lowered myself down to her, trying not to make sudden movements, but she thrashed about anyway honking like a goose.

"Calm now," I said, "come on." But she took no notice and things weren't helped by Dog, who raced up and down the edges of the drain barking shrilly.

She was in up to her armpits, and while I wrapped myself around her middle and pulled hard, she shifted only the smallest amount and when I let go the mud sucked her deeper. Her feet had already made holes for themselves and she farted back into them. I caught my breath and looked up at Dog who was still barking.

"Will you shut the fuck up, you arsehole?" I shouted, and he lay down and whined. I moved around the sheep and tried pulling one leg out at a time, but the rest of her sunk deeper in. I could feel the panic in her, and that I was hurting her. After fifteen minutes I was sweating and worried that if I left to get help, whatever that might be, she'd drown.

"Hi there." A shadow fell over me; it was him. I strengthened my grip on the sheep like I could use her to swing at him. Dog stood up and wagged his tail and for a moment I was speechless. The man looked at me down in the ditch. "I wondered if you could help me out." Sober, he had the voice of a news reader. He took a mobile phone out of his pocket. "There's no signal here—I was using the map but it's gone." He held the phone up and squinted like he was reading something from it. "I'm a bit stuck." He had dark rings around his eyes. He squinted at me. "It was you last night in the shed, wasn't it?" The ewe let out a wail. "I recognise your . . . hair." He cleared his throat. The blood in my calves was cut off by the weight of the sheep, but I could feel the pulse in my legs fast and heavy.

I swallowed. "I could really do with your help."

He suddenly looked like he might just run away. "With the sheep?"

"That's about what I was hoping." I tried to keep my voice steady but didn't manage it.

His arms hung at his sides. He clenched and unclenched his fists. "Won't it work its way free on its own?"

I felt the rattle of the sheep's heartbeat and she shifted her weight further down into the mud. I tried not to shout or swear.

"I need to get this sheep out," I said in a clear and careful way.

"You'll need to get that sheep out," Don called. I turned and saw him leaning against the fence at the top of the hill with a perfect view. He jabbed a finger towards the sheep. I gave Don the thumbs-up for a moment too long, and he gave me a double thumbs-up back, smiling broadly.

"Couldn't you ask that guy? It's just I don't know all that much about sheep. He looks like he would know an awful lot more."

"Please," I said. Teeth. "If you don't help me my sheep will drown in the mud."

A look of helplessness passed over his face, but he took his jacket off and laid it on the ground. He lowered himself down the bank. Dog got up and put his mudded undercarriage onto the jacket.

"Right," he said, and fell to his knees, landing with a smack in the mud. The sheep let out a horrified mew and wobbled about, straining to get away from him. He stood up, squelching.

"Right," he said again and tried to offer a hand to shake over the sheep. I looked at the hand; it was a large man's hand with

71

puncture wounds on it from Dog. I was glad my arms were underneath the sheep. He retracted the hand. "Name's Lloyd."

"Jake." I nodded at him and he clapped his hands loudly, making the sheep lurch forward, then rubbed them together.

"Where do you want me?"

The sheep foamed at the mouth.

"You're scaring the sheep."

"Right," he whispered.

"If you grab her around the back end, I'll get the front end."

"The back end," he repeated to himself. "Good."

I gripped her under the armpits and felt the give while I waited for him to prepare himself at the other end. It involved a lot of stretching and huffing. He kept looking like he was going to put his arms around her and then leaning away at the last minute into a shoulder stretch. Finally, and with his head straining away from the sheep, he got hold of her.

"You're doing well," Don crowed from up the hill.

"Right," Lloyd said. "Right."

"On the count of three, pull upwards, and keep hold of her."

"Right."

"One, two, three," and we both pulled and the ewe's legs sucked in the mud, and she popped out like a cork. She started to kick and tried to scramble, and before I could tell him to keep hold he let out a yell and fell backwards. The ewe kicked and kicked, horrified by the noise. She bored past my grip and I fell face first into the mud. Dog ran up and down the bank barking and rearing about. The ewe took about three leaps before getting stuck again. I dragged myself up and went over to where the man sat in the mud holding his chest, white and staring.

"What happened? Are you all right?" I said. He looked up at me with disbelief, and I thought, *Jesus, is he having a heart attack?* He puffed out, long and slow, and then started to cough again.

"I just didn't expect it to move that much." His eyes were watering. "They're so much bigger close up."

Up on the hill, I could hear Don laughing. "You'll need to give that another go!" he managed to croak out.

The man looked at me from his seat in the mud. "I think I might be afraid of sheep," he said.

10

Otto is watching his soaps with his sun-browned and knotted hands resting snugly on top of his groin. He's told me before that the heat those parts make is good for his arthritis. In the time I've been here, he's grown so used to me that on hot days like this he doesn't bother to put his shorts on.

I pretend to go out to the dunny, but instead, once I've made sure Kelly is not watching from her bed on the veranda, I nip into the tractor shed and peer into the open bonnet of Otto's spare truck, the truck that was supposed to be mine, which I know works, because I've heard the engine. It's greased all over and I have to be careful not to get any of it on me. I use a creosote-stained rag and I reach in and yank at the wires towards the back of the engine. I don't know what I am doing, and those could just be the wires that make the windscreen wipers go, and so I also take the monkey wrench that's resting on the edge of the bonnet and I take out three important-looking washers, cringing at every squeak they make. But I can hear the television spewing out of the house, and so really it's just Kelly I have to worry about. I think about taking the keys out of the ignition too, but I imagine Otto passing by and seeing them gone. At least with the engine, he might not see it straight away. There is nothing I can find that is sharp enough to pierce the tyres, so I have to leave it at that. When I come out of the shed, I turn away from the house and throw the washers one by one as far as I can into the tall dry grasses of the paddock where they can sink into the rest of the rusted scythes, the broken cages and the bicycle tyres. I can smell the carcasses of the sheep we killed last week, and I keep my gaze above the line of the grass, because yesterday, I caught sight of the ewe with the black-spotted nose while Kelly was moving her body around the place, deeper and deeper into the paddock. I rub my hands in the dirt to get rid of any trace of oil and then I count my steps back to the house, and it's my countdown, there's nothing to be done now, my hands have made the decision for me. I'll need to be gone by the next time Otto starts work on his truck. *Please god not today.*

I pass Kelly out on the veranda, on her rag rug, and she lifts her head to smell me as I go by. It's not a smell of *Hello*, it's a smell of *What are you up to?*

Back inside Otto looks up from *Shortland Street* and gives me a smile. He is always happiest at this time of day, with a full belly and a beer in his hand, the show on the TV, which I have to pretend to enjoy. A woman dressed as a nurse orders a lime and soda in a pub and my hands clench. I will go in the morning, that is when his old bones are slowest.

My night is sleepless, and I listen to Kelly snoring outside my window. She cries in her sleep. When the sky starts to lighten, I hear her get up and go and pee a little way from her sleeping ditch, and then I hear her slump herself back down for the final rest before the day. If she is awake, she watches the blue come into the sky, and a single bush curlew from another place cutting across the open spaces of the paddock. The flies start to thicken the air.

By the time Otto unlocks my door I have filled my pockets with everything I can carry without looking suspicious. Before I leave the room, I look at all of the things that need to stay behind and say goodbye to them. I slide the knife from under my bed into the very back of the cupboard, where it might never be found. Even after everything, I wouldn't want Otto to know I'd ever thought about slitting his throat.

I cook a breakfast of chops and eggs, and he wipes a slice of white bread around his plate and sighs happily. I force down an egg on a heel of bread, to look normal, but it starts to come back up, and I have to run to the loo and Otto rubs my back when I come out.

"Remember last week? Maybe it's the morning sicks," he says, hopefully. "When my mother was preggo with my little brother we had to give her meadowsweet just to keep water down. I'll pick some up when I'm next in town." Not: *when we're next in town*. That time has long passed. I wonder how long it would take for him to get me pregnant. Every time we finish, I squat in the shower and try to flush everything out.

"Roight," he says, slapping the meat of his gut, "to the day's business."

He scrapes back his chair and lays a large dry hand on my shoulder as he passes by. *The last time*, I think, and it sends a jolt through my belly, and when he thumps down the steps of the veranda, and heads out towards the dunny, throwing Kelly his chop bone as he goes, I feel a prickling on my skin. The key for the ute hangs over the oven and it catches the light. I take the can of money from under the sink, and the key from its hook, and I walk as calmly as I can out of the door. Kelly is chomping her bone, standing with her legs planted far apart, and she looks up at me from hooded eyes as I pass by, considering. I tell myself I am fetching something from the truck, so that if she can read my mind she won't know. But the second I slot the key into the ute's door, she drops the bone from her teeth and starts up, jumping on the spot with fury, loud loud loud.

The dunny door opens, and Otto crouches with his trousers around his ankles, a red face, his yellow legs bowed. I'm inside the ute and the door is closed, and the key is in the ignition. Kelly jumps at my window. I have to keep a calmness in me so that the truck doesn't stall, but Otto has left it in gear which I didn't notice, and so it does, and he has pulled up his trousers, and the panic is setting in on me, I'm already trying to think of an excuse, that I was practising my parking, or that I thought I'd drive up to the sheep, nothing I know that will wash, and Otto is running at me, shaking the rolled-up comic book he's been reading, like he's going to flog me on the nose with it; his face is an open hole of anger, and the truck starts again, and I jerk away from the dog, and Otto reaches me just in time to slam his whole body onto the bonnet and we look each other in the eye for the count of one and I know somehow that this will be it, that if he catches me, my body will end up in the tall dry grasses of the paddock, with Kelly shifting me deeper and deeper in every few days and the flies will blow me as I bloat up and the sun peels the skin from my bones.

I put the truck in reverse and Otto flops forward onto the ground, and there is a squeak from Kelly and I go backwards for a long time, until Otto is standing again, and running for the shed, and I have to hope the things I pulled out of the truck were the right things.

I turn myself around slowly, carefully, see Kelly in my wing mirror, lying on the ground, and despite everything, I feel bad, she is just a dog, and then I go, and I don't stop for the wooden gate, I smash through it, and it's so old, it flies off like it's made of paper. I turn left on the road towards town, and I keep going. I do not look in my rear-view mirror. I drive past the town, in case someone recognises the ute, and then I just drive fast, not seeing more than two cars by the time I have used up a third of a tank of diesel. I can go straight for as long as the truck will take me.

*   *   *

The air is different out here, the sour meat smell is gone, and I keep all the windows down, even though the wind bangs at my ears. The smell is not of old unwashed places or of fat and eggs frying, it is of hot leaves and earth and bitumen. I take as many sharp turns as I can, and wind my way through three or four small towns so that when he comes looking I can throw him off. I wonder in what way Otto will come after me, because I am certain that he will. There's a possibility that he might call the police, I guess, but the idea of a cell is not so bad. They don't know me out here.

When it feels like the sun has crisped my eyelids and it has started to edge down over west, I pull into a motel. I park badly across a set of lines, but no one else is in the parking lot so it doesn't seem to matter. The truck's engine ticks like a panting dog.

I ask the lady behind the counter if there's anywhere I can park that won't be seen from the road.

"You in some kind of trouble, missy?" she asks in not a nice way. Her hair is creeping out of the red handkerchief she wears on her head.

"I've left my boyfriend, I don't want him to find me."

"Been roughing you up, has he?" I nod, and the lady's face softens. "Well," she says, "pay up-front and I'll show you round to the back where Eddie keeps the boat."

I peel off three notes from the roll in Otto's tin and she's happy. Once I've parked, she gives me a key and also a bar of chocolate. "You drown your sorrows with that, missy," she says. "You get trouble, dial nine and I'll send Eddie round with a bat."

Eddie's boat is a speed boat with a shiny red hull. I am so far from the water, and I think of the smell of it, the winds and the chuck and gulp of water lapping at the fibreglass. I will drive to the coast tomorrow; I won't stop until I get there and I can float face down in the waves.

"It's never touched the bloody sea," says the woman, and reknots her hair into the handkerchief as she walks back to reception.

I buy three packets of smokes—they have the kind me and Karen used to smoke, Holidays, like that's going to trick you—a box of matches and a postcard with a photograph of a dolphin on it from the gas station, and I smoke a whole packet in my non-smoking room. I feel bad after the lady gave me the chocolate and let me park round the back, near Eddie's boat, but I'm not ready for the outside yet. I prop the postcard up on the pillow and use it as something to look at. It's hot as hell, and probably the cigarette smoke is not the most refreshing smell, but it feels so good and I push away the memory of Otto's red little penis.

After the smokes, I have a long hot shower and get into bed still wet so that the ceiling fan will cool me off while I sleep. I dream of the sheep out there alone with Otto and Kelly, and start up in the night with my heart pounding wondering what will happen to them. I sleep again but wake at dawn to throw up over and over into the loo, like I'm turning inside out, getting rid of the chops and the dog hair, Otto's tongue and Kelly's mackerel breath. I drink water from the tap in the way Mum used to shout at us for, in case the spider was up there nesting. I drink long hard gulps of it. I watch the day come while I smoke a Holiday and the birds sing and everything smells brand-new.

In a servo someone has left behind a newspaper called *Shearing World*. I get a cup of black coffee and a juice and flick through the paper. There's a column at the back where they advertise for work, and where people advertise themselves as wanting work.

Almost every one has a tick by "Experienced." I can hold a bloody sheep, and I can take its fleece off. Yes, I think, fuelled by the coffee and reaching for my Holidays. I pick a place that sounds busy, and that is far away, Kalgoorlie, and I buy a map in the servo so I can find it. It is nearly two thousand kilometres if I drive to the coast. I also buy three litres of tropical juice and two litres of water. My money should last, I can take my time getting down to Kalgoorlie if I want. Otto has been surprisingly good at saving, there's more money than I was expecting in the tin. I wonder if I should have just taken half. It makes me think again how if he does find me he'll kill me.

On my way, I stop now and again to look at how the land changes. The further south I get the redder things are. I get to the coast in the early morning, after a drive through the night, and tread out in the flat water at Monkey Mia. It smells familiar and good. There's a sign that says SWIM WITH THE DOLPHINS, and about a dozen tourists wearing orange life jackets bob around in the water at the end of a pier. I'm stunned at seeing so many people all at once. A smallish fin flits between them and I can hear them laughing apart from one young girl who screams because she's terrified. And she should be, that orange'll be visible to any passing darkness, not just the dolphins. I walk away from them up the beach, far out from the shore, but somehow the water only ever reaches my calves, not deep enough to swim in. Right on the point, a pod of dolphins, sixteen or so of them, come in close to me, and I can see their slick rounded backs and their blow-holes as well as their fins. I wave my arms about; partly I am waving hello and partly I want them not to come too close.

Back inland, at an empty truck stop, there's a goanna on the picnic table and I sit for a while on a rock nearby and watch him. When I stand up he darts off the table, and rizzles into the scrub.

There's a dunny at the picnic area, but just going near it sets off a bloom of blue bottles and the smell is a familiar one. I go in the scrub and say sorry out loud to the goanna.

I park up on the side of the road, because I'm too tired to keep going the hour and half to the next servo marked on the map. But it's a jumpy night, and even though Otto doesn't know what direction I went in, I turn the engine back on, drive onto the plain and park behind a lump of flowering scrub for a bit of protection. The doors are locked and then I sleep deeply, curved to the shape of the truck's seats, with the handbrake butting my ribs. I wake before dawn and there's a small dingo not far from the truck, he's got his paws around the back leg of something that died a long time ago, and he's chowing down happily. My stomach moves inside me, and hurts. It's probably time I ate something. I swig on the last of the tropical juice and decide not to ever drink it again, three litres is too much.

When I reach the next servo, everything smells of cooked meat, and it takes me such a long time to choose something to eat, the lady behind the till gets itchy.

"Something you can't find, doll?" I jump.

"I just can't decide." And I flush because it sounds like I think I'm choosing a wedding ring. I find a salad roll tucked away in a corner of the fridge and pick up a bag of cheese twists and a Coke.

"After all that," says the lady, but now I'm up close to her I can see she's not trying to be a bitch, and I smile. "You'd better have one of those on the house," she says like she's poured me a whisky. She's added a chocolate Freddie the Frog to my toddler's meal. I catch sight of myself in the window as I go to sit down and I am thin and even in the reflection I can see the dark shadows under my cheekbones. I save the Freddie the Frog until it melts in the glove compartment. He represents something I'm not sure I understand.

*   *   *

81

When I see kangaroos I am so surprised I don't slow or swerve or do anything other than watch as they bound past the bonnet of the car, and I catch one on the hindquarters and it flies up in the air like I've made it into a different creature by hitting it. It comes down and when it lands it doesn't just lie there dead, it's on its feet before I can even stop the truck, and it is gone into the low brush faster even than it was moving before. I sit watching, my hands wrapped hotly around the steering wheel, my heart bouncing at my gullet. I can't believe it just got up and went, I was going at least ninety. I laugh out loud at how wonderful life is that it takes a hell of a knock like that and it's just fine, and I find the steadiness in myself and get out of the car to check the damage. The fender is dented, but there is nothing to be done about that, and the paintwork has gone, through to the body. I look up at the roo as she bounds mightily away, but all at once she stops mid-bound, and her legs fly out from under her, spazzing, like she's caught on an electric fence. She drops and lurches up again, her legs going every which way, her small arms stretched at the sky, her claws splayed like stars, and the dust flying all around. The others are just blurs in the distance now, and she is going mad, I can hear her body smack the earth every time she lands. I don't let my thoughts touch the sides as I take the crowbar out of the toolbox in the back of the truck and I cross over the empty road.

All I let myself think walking through that scrub towards her is that I am capable, I am strong in the arm and so is my crowbar. She is all over the place, there is blood coming from somewhere, which is all around the clearing she has made in the scrub. Her eyes roll and her thrashing makes a wind at my face. I wish my crowbar was a rifle. I watch her head, wait for it to come around with her twitching, which has slowed, and when it comes towards me I raise the crowbar high in the air, picturing the sheep with the black spots on its nose and thinking, *You are capable*, and I bring it down with everything in me onto the side of her head, and there is a crunch—I've broken through which is good news for both of us in the long term. Her juddering slows, but there is still movement, and quickly I bring it down again and again until long after she has stopped her twitching and until there is really not much of a head left.

I take a step back. Behind me I hear something coming on the highway and when I look it's a road train. It honks loudly at the sight of my truck, which is not pulled over and is in the middle of the road, but he doesn't slow down; instead he crosses to the other side to pass it, but not enough that he doesn't take off my wing mirror. Even from here I can hear a voice laughing from inside the cab as my wing mirror bounces and then smashes on the bitumen.

11

Inside, while Lloyd sat on the sofa, I'd filled a mug with water. He drank it and then held his forehead in his hands. I washed the mud off my face and dried it with a tea towel. Outside rattled against the windows. I turned the kitchen light on and it flickered on and off and on again.

I wondered how old he was—younger than my father the last time I'd seen him, but older than the farmers who came to offer their services. I took mugs out of the cupboard and put them back. I found a pack of paracetamol and set them on the counter, wondering if I should offer them to him, or if that would encourage him to stay. I watched him from the corner of my eye, watched for a look or a sudden movement. I ran an itinerary of the kitchen. Hammer under the sink, half a brick on the window sill.

"I told you in the woolshed that someone's been killing my sheep," I said with my back to him.

"Oh dear," he said. "I'm sorry, last night's a bit patchy." I turned around to look at him. He smiled. "Er, do you think they're doing it on purpose?" I held his gaze.

"Yes."

He didn't turn away, but after a while, when I suppose it got awkward, he smiled and cleared his throat. I handed him the paracetamol, more to break the stillness than anything else.

"This is so kind of you," he said. "Thank you." He popped out four of the pills and chewed them, with a long gulp of water afterwards.

"How many sheep do you have?" he asked, and looked pleased to have thought of a question.

"Fifty. But I lost two this month, so less."

"What's getting them? A fox?"

"Maybe. Might be kids. Might be someone else." He looked relaxed like he'd always been sitting there, like we were old friends, like he knew what would happen next and nothing was out of the ordinary.

"Kids? Jesus." He smiled. "When I was a kid the worst we got up to was stealing cigarettes and liquorice."

"Well."

"You really think kids would be capable of something like that?"

I picked up my mug of water and drank but didn't answer. Lloyd stopped talking. The wind screamed down the pipe of the Rayburn and soot scuttled down the chimney.

"I'll give you a lift into town," I said, and Lloyd looked up. He glanced out the window.

"Oh, right. Sure—that's good of you." He made no move to get up, so I picked my keys out of my pocket and shook them to make the sound of leaving. Even Dog remained sitting. Lightning flash with thunder dead on top.

"If we go now, I'll be able to . . ." I trailed off, not quick enough to think of a reason, but holding my keys out.

"Oh, sure, now?" He looked out the window again. "Is it safe you think? To drive in?"

"It's just weather."

"Sure, sure." He stood, creaking under his breath. He patted Dog on the head. "No hard feelings, eh?" he said to him and Dog narrowed his eyes in a friendly way. I wondered a moment what he planned on doing that would give Dog hard feelings.

"He's coming with us," I said.

"Righto."

Rain blasted against the window. I struggled to open the front door, the wind was now possibly a gale.

"Hoo!" said Lloyd, and the three of us ran to the truck.

In the driver's door was the short metal spirit level I'd found in the shed—sharp edges, heavy, and I knew it fit closely in the palm of my hand. When Lloyd closed the door on the passenger side, the truck felt smaller, like he'd used up all the air. My left side burnt with being close to him. I would drive with one eye on him and if he reached out I could brake suddenly—the seatbelt on his passenger side had lost its retractor, and so it just hung there loosely. He would be catapulted into the dashboard. And then I'd have the spirit level. I looked at Dog in the back seat—I'd just have to hope he was lying down at the time.

With the wipers on full, I could catch glimpses of the track, between the rain and dead leaves and twigs. As we came over the crest of the hill, the truck shook as the wind hit us side on.

"Oooh," said Lloyd and his arm came up and I jumped and looked at him. He jumped too, but he was only bracing himself against the ceiling. He craned to look out of his window.

"What did you see?"

"Nothing."

A beech had fallen over the track which would lead us to the woods and out onto the road. Lloyd sucked air through his teeth. I didn't slow down, we would go around it, because this was exactly the kind of thing a four-wheel-drive vehicle was built for.

"Gosh," said Lloyd and looped his other hand through the door handle. I stopped and clunked the gear stick into four-wheel drive and the engine took on its deeper growl and I ground us off the road and into the field with the truck bouncing from side to side and Lloyd saying over and over, "Gosh" and "Hoo" every time the truck rocked. "Right!" he said loudly as we powered at the incline that would get us back up onto the road, and it was then that I knew we wouldn't make it, the empty sound of the wheels spinning without purchase, of the truck sinking deeper into its hole, digging itself in, relaxing and staying put. I revved the engine until the air stank. The windows fogged. I hit the steering wheel and closed my eyes and shouted, "Shit and fuck and balls," and in the silence afterwards, Lloyd said,

"Whoops. Stuck in the mud. Been a lot of that today."

The water still ran, and steam made it out from under the door while Lloyd showered in the downstairs bathroom. I scanned the spare room. There were sheets that had been left in the cupboard when I moved in, and I made what I decided was a bed that was not welcoming, but adequate. Good enough for one night but not encouraging a long stopover. The blanket was itchy at any rate. He had helped with the sheep, I reminded myself. He had pushed the truck when I'd asked him too, had taken a face full of mud and had suggested filling the trenches the wheels had dug with sticks for grip, but we had only sunk deeper. It was a job for Don and his towbar, another mark in the incompetency column, but when we'd got back to the house, freezing and soaked, Don hadn't answered the phone.

I opened the window as an afterthought; the room smelled of damp and dust. Dead moths blew in from the window sill, and I scooped them into my hand, suddenly embarrassed.

When Lloyd came out of the bathroom, he had the towel wrapped around his midriff. I tried not to look at the bare parts of him, but that was the larger part. There was a lot of hair on his chest, some of it grey. He ambled towards me and I felt a horror that the towel might drop.

"Is there somewhere I could wash these?" he asked, holding up his mud-soaked clothes. "Or even just dry them?"

"I can put them in the wash," I said, but my voice came out in a squeak I wasn't expecting. I cleared my throat and spoke in a voice that was deeper than my own. "And then they can dry on the radiator."

"If it's not too much bother," he said, "thanks so much. Feeling better already." He smiled. I frowned, and turned away.

He sauntered around the room in his towel, looking at the pictures that hung on the walls. "These yours?" he said, pointing at one of a set of men in uniform.

"Here when I moved in."

He had an annoying habit of flexing the calf that showed through the gap in the side of the towel.

"They belong to Don—I bought the place off him."

Lloyd nodded and made a mooing noise. "He left them for you?"

"I guess."

"Huh."

I wasn't sure what he meant by that, but it was something annoying. Would we just sit there and wait until his clothes were clean and dry? I tried calling Don again. There was no answer. It was getting late—if he didn't answer soon, it meant he was staying the night in town. I tried to calculate the time we would spend waiting for the storm to pass, for night to be over, for Don to come home and answer his phone.

"Would you like something to eat?"

Lloyd looked at me and so did Dog. "I—I hate to put you out."

"Well," I said.

I put the same stew on the stove I'd been heating the night

before. Lloyd sighed and sat heavily on the sofa. I watched him out of the corner of my eye, knew that the sigh of comfort was in fact an intake of breath through pain, because he had thrown himself down on the dividing bar of the sofa where it was hard and broken. I turned my back, pretended not to notice him do it, but I could see him in the reflection of the window. He rubbed the sore spot on his lower back and Dog clambered up next to him and Lloyd fondled his ears. I forced my shoulders to drop.

Lloyd's leg peeped out of its towel again, flexing. He leant his head on his arm so that I saw his armpit. I went to the cupboard and found a dressing gown Don had also left behind. I put it on the side of the sofa.

"You can wear this," I said and went back to the stove.

"Lovely," he said and when I turned around he was tying it up, his wet hair now done up with the towel in a turban. The dressing gown had belonged to Don's wife, I assumed. It had a trail of daisies down both lapels and a trim of cartoon mice. Lloyd sat down a little more carefully and he said, "Very nice," quietly to himself.

The time passed slowly.

"Would you like a drink?" I blinked at myself.

"If it's not too much of an imposition," he said, "that would be so lovely."

I poured him some whisky and he held his glass with both hands as he lifted it to his mouth.

I sat at the kitchen table and he sat on the sofa and every now and then he sighed in a way that was supposed to seem like the start of a conversation. We drank our whisky; I drank mine quickly because every time the silence became uncomfortable, I took another sip.

"So," he said eventually, "I suppose you're wondering what I'm doing up here?"

I didn't reply, just watched him. He shuffled forward and put his glass down on the floor next to his foot. "Look," he said in a tone that was too warm and comforting for my liking, "I just thought it might make you feel a little odd that I just turned up." His voice went up at the end, like he had an accent I hadn't noticed before. I sat up straight.

"Where are you from?" I said, with more aggression than the question needed. He frowned.

"Originally?"

"Are you from Australia?"

"Barnsley. My mother's from Stockton, my father from Leeds. I grew up in Barnsley. I live in London." And the accent was gone, just a trick of my ear. I settled back down in my chair. There was a silence. "And you—obviously—*are* from Australia." And then it came: "What brought you to the island?"

"Sheep."

"Oh?" he said in a way that meant I was supposed to carry on talking. Instead I got up and poured another drink. After a second's thought I decided it was more out of the ordinary and awkward not to pour him one too, so I refilled his glass. He looked up and smiled. Drink made men dark but it also made them sloppy. I added water to mine.

The stew had cooked too long and stuck to the pot. I put two bowlfuls out on the table with the bread.

Lloyd took the towel off his head and shook out his hair, which dried into waves, grey around his ears.

I searched for a moment for a bread knife and remembered it was still upstairs.

"I'm out of knives for the time being," I said, "so you'll have to tear the bread, and spread butter with the back of a spoon." Lloyd nodded like this was not unusual.

12

It's so hot I feel as though I'll bloat up and explode like a dead possum, and after checking the sheep, I find myself on my bike, with wind through my hair. The feeling that Otto won't know exactly where to find me takes hold and I keep going. I cycle into the mirage, can feel the sun flaying my back and shoulders, the lids of my eyes, but it's worth it to feel like I'm en route to something. I imagine finding a waterhole that's not dried up in the drought; I think over and over, I'll just ride to the end of this mirage, but there's nothing here. I don't know how long I've been gone, but I become aware of the heat in a new way. Thirst comes and then goes again. The mirage is replaced by black and red stars. All I want to do is keep going, if it takes a week of riding, if the sun kills me, I want to be at the coast, I want to open my eyes in the water to see the deep cool nothing below the surface and to let the tide take me where it likes. Away.

I come off the bike when I hit a rock, and it throws me over the handlebars. Apart from skin off my knees and hands, I'm fine, but it's hard to get up. There's a shrub that casts a small shadow and I wheel myself over to it, and slump there. There is salt on my lips, I am thirsty and burnt, but not unhappy. I lie there and watch a whistler high up, riding the hot air, and I imagine it is a seagull and I am in the bottom of a boat, jumping with sea lice. Karen is with me, we're drinking Cokes and she's got her fingers laced through mine. I will stay here, I think, I will pull up the anchor and lie in the hull of the boat and let it take me to wherever the centre is.

I walk down the corridor of my brain and don't even look at the doors either side.

When I wake up, Otto is standing over me, his face a rage. He picks me up, puts me over his shoulder, and the feeling is of my sunburnt skin being pulled off. A taste of what it is like to be burnt, properly.

When I wake a second time, I am in my bed and Otto is feeding water into my mouth, and then he rubs cream into my back and over my face. "Bloody disgrace," I hear him say.

The next morning I have a fever and the room spins. Otto isn't talking to me, just comes in with a sandwich now and again, stands over me till I eat it, until I am well again. When I feel well again, I come out of my bedroom in a towel and Otto is there in the living room watching the soaps. He doesn't look at me.

"Well," he says to the TV, "the princess awakes."

"I got lost," I say.

"Got lost in a straight line? That'd take some doing."

"I was looking for a waterhole," but while I'm trying to think up a story, my eyes catch on something out the front of the house, and I trail off. My bike is lying on its side, wrecked. It has been driven over repeatedly, squashed flat into the ground.

"My bike" is all I can say.

Otto looks at me. "I didn't see it," he says, and he doesn't even try to make me believe him.

Later that night, I am in my room and he unlocks my door, lies down next to me and wants sex, but I don't want anything to do with him. I am angry and I push him away.

"What's this?" he asks.

"I don't want to."

"You sulking?" I don't reply. "You're lucky I don't beat the hell out of you with the back of a brush, girly," he says and stands up. From the doorway he says, "You don't fool me." And then he slams the door and makes a point of locking it noisily. I hear him go to the living room and put the TV on. The fridge door closes and shakes the house.

In the morning, he greets me with a grim look in his eye.

"Low on meat" is all he says and he takes me by the wrist to the truck, where Kelly is already waiting, panting with excitement. We drive out to the sheep and from the back of the truck he brings a heavy black canvas bag. I think about the shoe under the house. The earring in the woolshed. The things Kelly finds to eat in the tall dry grass.

Otto grips a ewe with a dreadful kind of strength I haven't seen before—like he's been keeping his muscles in hibernation until this point. It is different from the strength he uses when he is shearing—it's cruel, like he wants her to know what's coming. He swings her up the ramp in front of him, and she gives out a terrible sound, and I stand there outside the woolshed, mute. Kelly is also silent; she crouches low to the ground by Otto's side, slinking here and there with those cloudy eyes and a look of a snake about her. The rest of the sheep have their ears forward and are backed into the far corner of the pen. *One by one*, they must be thinking, and I tackle the urge to kick down the fence and tell them to flee. They will only stand there. From where I am, I can see into the woolshed, the hook with its dark stain beneath it.

"Get in here, girl, I want you to see how it's done," shouts Otto, and I pretend I can't hear him, because I can't move. I see him shake his head and the sheep's cries rattle my bones. He takes a wide-bladed knife from his bag and slices once across the white throat of the sheep and she is still alive and trying to bleat. Otto holds her firm between his thighs, and her back legs are going like crazy and the red comes out of her neck like a tap has been turned on. He cuts again and her voice fades out into a gurgle as he goes through the windpipe, and the stamp of her hooves weakens. There is a scream in me that wants to come out, but I won't let it, I won't look away.

Otto drops the ewe, who still moves, but softly, she is not going anywhere, and only now does Kelly start to bark, baring her teeth close to the sheep's eye which is rolling back, showing the white; the dog lunges again and again at the sheep, not biting, just snapping at the air near her face. I hear my name shouted again and I follow, and inside the woolshed is the smell of new blood.

"You need to learn how it's done." He wipes his forearm under his nose to get rid of the sweat, and leaves a streak of brown blood on his face. He stares at me, an unbroken gaze that prickles the hair on my neck. There's something about him in the blood fug that is natural. A bird squawks from on top of the shed. Otto shrugs and the tension breaks. "No matter, we'll do another." My knees weaken.

The sheep is dead now, and Kelly drools over it; no longer concerned with scaring it, she's waiting to be given a taste. Otto takes a smaller knife and cuts the tendons at the sheep's back ankles before poking some hooks in and hoisting her off the floor with a pulley and rope. I see a bead of blood land in her open eye.

"And that's how them Muslims do it," he says, a smile of satisfaction on his face. He cuts off one of her front feet and gives it to Kelly, who accepts the hoof like it has always belonged to her. She stands, legs apart, and grinds her teeth into it.

"Right," says Otto, "go and grab one then." I stand still. "Come on, get a move on."

"I can't," I say.

"I've seen you pick a sheep up. Come on," says Otto, "don't be wet."

"I don't want to."

Otto looks at me through a narrowed eye. "Part of having animals, girl. I told Carole about this, an' she didn't listen either. Didn't pick you out as being spooked by a bit of blood." There's a small smile around his lips; he's trying not to show it but he is amused, and he is enjoying seeing me scared.

I can feel my strong arms floating from my shoulders, as weak as feathers. I want to do something to make him understand that it is important that this doesn't happen. I am sorry for my bad behaviour, I want to tell him, I want to say I won't do it again, I promise. I will take the beating with a brush, but not this. But all I can make is the word "Please."

He stomps out of the shed and comes back with a wild-eyed sheep, the one with black spots on her nose. Otto has a smile on his face, he's let it out, doesn't care what I know about him. He looks at me like I'm a kid who's thrown a tantrum and he is going to teach me a lesson and then laugh about it afterwards. It is going to happen regardless of how much I don't want it to happen, and I can see he has a hard-on through his shorts, and he is doing this because he likes me best when I'm small and like a child and he can tuck me into bed and feed me with a spoon and I see the horrible certainty of the challenge, and I will show him that I am stronger than he thinks, and the sheep with the black spots on her nose will be the sacrifice.

Somewhere a tarpaulin flaps in a breeze that doesn't reach me. I reel it in just as the tears have filled my eyes, I blink them back inside, and take the knife from the boards, where it is still hot and red from the last sheep, and the ewe with the black spots is whipping about underneath Otto, and Kelly has stopped crunching her sheep's foot and is watching, interested as I transfer the sheep between my legs and pull her head back to expose her throat. I clamp a hand over her black-spotted nose so she can't make those terrible sounds any more, and in one motion I cut her throat, as deep and hard as I can, I want her to be dead before she knows about it, but she still writhes about under me as blood pours out of her, and as her strength goes, so does mine, but I hold her to me, I press my face into the wool at the back of her head. Kelly is barking again. Otto is silent and watching, and he glances at the knife I'm still holding, his smile gone.

Once Otto has taken off the ribs and shoulders, we dump the carcasses out in the paddock next to the house, and Kelly high-steps it next to us, animated and puppy-like. We don't throw them far in, and she goes and bites and bites again at what is left. I wish he had taken the heads off. Kelly goes down on her shoulder and rolls on the remains. We have sex almost immediately as we get back in the house and I let him do what he wants with me, which is everything. Afterwards, when he's gone, I drop to the floor and do push-ups until I see black dots.

In the morning, after my shower, I'm standing over the bathroom sink and my eyes fall on Otto's eardrops. Without giving myself a chance to think, I take off the lid and pour them down my throat. Otto comes in to find me heaving into the toilet.

"What's the matter, pet?"

I feel crook, but I ham it up anyway.

"I need to go to the hospital." Once I'm there I can slip away, or tell someone, a kind-looking nurse, that I have to get away from him, I picture her helping me into her car and driving me to the station, giving me money for a ticket to the coast. Otto feels my forehead as I'm spewing. I will it to be hot.

"It hurts," I say, clutching my stomach. I want to give him the idea of a burst appendix. Otto runs his hand over his face.

"Look," Otto says finally, "I'll go into town and get you something to settle your stomach."

"I need to see a doctor."

"You'll be right." He goes to leave.

"I want to see a doctor, I'm really sick," I say, making my voice as weak as I can, but Otto has made up his mind, I can see it on his liver-spotted face.

"I'll get you some medicine. You've just had too much sun again," he says in a way that I know to be the final word.

I listen to Otto's truck drive away without me. I'd imagined myself drinking a Coke and buying some more Holidays, smoking one in a gas station.

I've thrown up all the drops, but I keep thinking of the wax inside Otto's ears; I know it was only the drops I swallowed, but it feels like his wax is coating me on the inside. I go to breathe some fresh air, but Kelly sits silently on the other side of the screen door, watching my movements. I flick her the bird but she is not impressed.

In Otto's bedroom there's a picture on the wall of a bunch of purple flowers in a pale yellow vase, but that is the only concession to decoration in the place. It's from another person, Carole probably. I never come in here, not even to clean—he always comes to me in my room, and the smell of the place is like he keeps a bowl of stew under his bed.

In the wardrobe I find a moth-eaten suit with a yellow stiffness around the armpits, and four dresses that would have belonged to a tiny woman. Below them are three small lady's shoes: two purple wedges and a single pink stiletto. All three have a deadly point that I can't imagine getting a single toe into. I stare at the pink shoe on its own. Out the bedroom window

I catch movement in the paddock, but it's probably just a bandi-coot or a rat. I hold my breath and watch, but nothing comes out of the tall dry grass.

Up on a shelf above the dresses is a chocolate box with no lid, in it the driver's licence of Carole McKinney from Carnarvon—it puts her age at forty-two. There are two bracelets made of blue and orange coral and a pink lipstick without its top. Underneath these objects is a large colour photograph of Carole and Otto on their wedding day. Otto is wearing the suit with the armpit stains and has Kelly standing next to him, staring straight into the camera. Otto's arm is around Carole's shoulders, so the armpit is visible. Carole wears one of the dresses that hangs in front of me—it's over the top, purple and with one shoulder bare, the other with a large satin bow on, like Carole is a present that is ready for unwrapping. She holds a small white hairy-looking dog with both hands. Her hair is in a short permed bob and has yellowish highlights all through it, her eyes are barely visible beneath the layers of mascara she wears, and there's that hot-pink lipstick, just about holding in her astonishing buck teeth. Carole is smiling, trying to keep the teeth in check, and she is presenting one long brown leg for the camera. Otto stands firm on both feet, straight-backed with a look that could bake biscuits. All of this is going on outside Darwin Registry Office. My hands start to sweat when I recognise the earrings Carole is wearing, and I have to put the photograph back in the box so I don't mark it. I would like to tear it up.

I go into the kitchen and I take out the box under the sink which is filled with rusted can openers and bent spoons. I find a curved boning knife, and go to put the box back under the sink. In the space behind where the box normally lives is a golden syrup tin I've never noticed before. I lever up its lid with a spoon and inside is a thick roll of money. I put it and the box back, and then I put the knife down the side of my bed. I lie down on the bed and think about that money, about how far it would go. There's the sound of Otto's truck coming up the drive. He brings me a can of Coke and some peppermint syrup.

13

I woke up early and lay a minute in bed trying to put things in the right order. I'd got into bed and lain there listening out for creaks on the stairs. None came and I had listened for the hammering on the wall, but it was quiet too. Something had changed in the house. Even the fox stopped shrieking. I'd slept deeply, not dreaming. When I woke, there were large beads of rain on the window, and the glass boomed now and again in its frame, but the sky was not deep brown any more. I could see the hedgerow at the top of the hill flattened by the wind.

Downstairs Lloyd was asleep on the sofa, an old Bible open on his chest. He'd left the lamp on and when I pressed the button to turn it off he snapped awake.

"Christ," he said, holding his hand up to his face. I picked up the phone and dialled Don's number. Still no reply. I was late—he might have come and gone already. I turned round and looked at Lloyd and his Bible.

"You god squad?" I said. He kept his hand over his eyes a few moments. When he took it away, he looked at me.

"What?" he said, then looked down at the Bible. "Oh."

I started to fill the kettle.

"No—the only book I could find, and I thought I'd give it a go." He yawned extravagantly.

"How was it?"

"It beat lying awake listening to you."

I stopped scraping. "Listening to what?"

"Jesus, you were having some kind of horror-film dream. I went up, thought you were being murdered, but the dog wouldn't let me in. You were shouting away, didn't wake up when I called out your name."

"I have to go and look after the sheep now," I said. Then I turned and walked back up the stairs to my room. The bath was filled to the brim with water. I pulled out the plug and watched it start to drain away. I dried my hands on a towel and went downstairs and stood in front of Lloyd.

"I have to go and look after the sheep now," I said again.

All sheep were accounted for, and the cold air burnt my lips and took the white smoke of breath from my mouth. There was a new smell to the day, the wind had changed direction and it brought with it salt and bonfires. Snowdrops that had come up in the night were pinned to the earth by the wind. I marked the sheep that looked like they had triplets and twins and Dog chased a rabbit into the woods.

I crutched a dozen or so of the furthest along, and while I worked, a fox appeared at the edge of the woods. I stopped what I was doing and watched her. Compared to the sheep she was small and skittish.

"It wasn't you, was it?" I asked out loud. If I was any kind of farmer, I'd be there with my gun and I'd take her out. I watched two skinny cubs amble up behind her. They were far too early, and she'd be needing food to keep her milk up, to keep her strength up. I looked at the ewe I'd just crutched, settled comfortably in the grass, saw her sigh at the solidness of herself against earth.

One of the fox cubs snapped at a fly, and the vixen's ears sprung around at something in the undergrowth. She kept one foot off the ground to listen, then hauled up a cub by its scruff and the other followed her back into the dark where it was safe. Dog appeared

101

out of the woods, long pink tongue lolling out of him, seeds plastered to his snout and goosegrass tangled around his back leg. He looked happy. If they could they would all kill each other, the fox would kill the sheep and then Dog would kill the fox.

Dog came up and smelled the newly sheared bum wool and then lay down panting heavily next to the pregnant sheep, who laboured up and moved away like she couldn't take the smell of him. From the trees a flock of starlings took off. Maybe they signalled the vixen moving deeper into the woods.

From the stile, I saw Don's truck was back and breathed a sigh of relief.

"Christ's neck, what happened to you?" he said as he opened the door, smiling like he always did when he knew exactly what had gone on and was waiting for me to ask for help. "Get bogged did you?"

"Could you give me a tow out?" I said, reddening.

"Good opportunity to call on one of those younger farmers, don't you think?" he said, making no move to get his boots on.

"I could do it myself if you'd let me have your keys. I could pull it out myself."

"Really? And who'd steer? Some things you just can't do on your own." He turned and started to pull on his oilskin. "That's why farmers need to know each other, you help them, they help you, that's just how it goes. All it'd take'd be the pub once a week for a couple of hours"—he started to push his feet into his gumboots—"because sooner or later I'm going to hit the post and be dead and then what'll you do? Starve to death I suppose." Don was in a good mood at least.

It took just a couple of tries to get the truck out, and when it was free, Don leant out his window. "This that chap who helped you out of the ditch?"

102

Lloyd was coming up the track, looking like a country rambler with an ash pole to help him along.

"Yep."

"Handy to have him around."

Lloyd raised a hand in hello. Don nodded back and turned his engine off. I turned mine off too, reluctantly.

"Hi there," said Lloyd to Don. He looked at me and I might have imagined it but he looked a little hurt. "I was wondering where you'd got to—thought I might be able to help? But you've got the car out I see." There was a quiet in which Lloyd's words hung.

Don looked back to me. "I'll come by with a chainsaw and get rid of this for you," he said, nodding at the tree.

"Thanks, but I've got a saw, I'll be right." Don narrowed his eyes at me.

"My saw's a big one," he said.

I nodded. "Mine's pretty big too."

"You know how to use it?"

"I do."

"Well," Don said, not satisfied. I curled my tongue into my mouth and gave a short smile. It was important not to be rude. Don turned his attention to Lloyd.

"Nice to see her with a bit of company about the place."

I cleared my throat.

"Oh," said Lloyd, visibly uncomfortable, "I'm afraid I rather forced myself on her."

Don barked, "About time!" He started up his engine so that he had the last word, raised a hand and disappeared up the track. Lloyd looked at me and I tried to soften my jaw.

"He likes winding you up that old guy, huh?"

"He does."

We drove back to get the chainsaw in silence. I went into the shed and topped up the diesel, and picked up an axe too. Lloyd waited by the car talking softly to Dog. I put the axe and chainsaw in the back and he moved to get in with me.

"You stay here," I said.

"Er—"

"With the dog." I got in the truck and left him there looking embarrassed.

Back at the fallen tree, I got out of the truck, left the door open and took the tools from the back. I started with the axe, feeling the fluid pump through my shoulders, skimming off the smaller branches until I had a clear shot at the trunk and then I laid into it, hacked with no particular aim, but a steady rhythm, shouting and sweating as I gouged at the wood until there was no strength left in my arms and I stopped to pant and close my eyes. I had the singular clear thought, *He doesn't know me.* And I pulled the choke out on the saw, and yanked the cord to start it.

It was dark by the time I was done, and raining. Lloyd had lit a fire in the fireplace.

"I hope you don't mind," he said when I walked in to find him standing at the sink, washing up. Dog wagged his tail from his spot on the sofa by the fire, like it was normal.

"How'd it go with the tree? I would have cooked something," he said, "but I didn't know what you were saving. I did a bit of cleaning instead." He turned around and looked at me. "Not because the place needed it, just to say thank you." He turned back to the sink.

"Huh," I said. It was annoying that he had moved things, and that the place looked nicer because of it. It smelled different, the air was dry and warm. I never lit the fire. I ran a bath and was in it before I noticed how much I ached.

104

We shared a can of mushroom soup at the table. I'd thought I could cook the chicken, but it smelled green. The wind rattled in the pipe of the Rayburn. It was late to take him into town, but maybe after tea.

"So," Lloyd said, not for the first time, and then because the silence was not comfortable, I got up and took a bottle of whisky out of the cupboard. I poured two mugs and sat down, handing one to him.

"Thank you," he said and coughed. "So."

Dog growled. We both looked over to him. He had left the warmth of the fire and was standing by the front door, head down. Lloyd looked at me.

"Why's he doing that?"

I scraped back my chair and went to the window.

"He can smell something outside." The growl was a deep one from down in his guts. I pulled back the curtain and looked out.

"Turn the light off," I said quietly.

Lloyd flipped the switch and came to stand next to me. I closed my eyes for a moment to try and get them used to the dark, then looked again.

"The human eye senses movement before all else," said Lloyd, and I stared at him. "What?" he said. "I read it in *National Geographic*."

Out the window, nothing moved.

"Someone's watching the house, I can feel it," I said, and Lloyd's eyes widened at me.

There was a loud knock at the door, and Dog bared his teeth and growled like a wolf.

"Fuck," we both whispered.

"Who's there?" called Lloyd in a deeper voice than I'd heard him use before. He coughed with his mouth closed.

There was no answer, but the doorknob started to turn and rattle like someone was trying to get in.

I went towards the door.

"What are you doing?" hissed Lloyd.

"This is stupid," I hissed back. "Hold Dog." Lloyd grabbed him by the scruff and held on while he barked and wrestled about. If I had been on my own, I would have taken the axe handle to the door with me.

On the other side of the door was a man with a young face. His hair was gelled in neat rows from his crown to where it spiked over his eyes in mouse-brown spears. Wind came into the house and all I could think about was a time in the near future when this man would be gone and the door would be closed and the wind was outside again.

"What do you want?" I asked in a voice that was not as confident as I had hoped. He looked at me, confused. It looked like his hair interfered with his eyes, which were red and crusted with yellow. The skin around his chin and neck had been recently picked free of spots. He wore a slick-looking puffer jacket, and he stared at me, rubbing his index finger up the side of his nose. He sniffed hard.

"Who are you?" he asked. He looked around me in a way that made me think he was about to come inside. Dog barked behind me.

"I live here," I said. "What do you want?" He stopped rubbing his nose and looking over my shoulder, and looked at me a few beats.

"Where's me dad?" asked the man.

"Are you— Do you mean Don?"

"I mean me dad and who the fuck are you?" His eyebrows drew together.

"I live here," I said again. "I bought this place off Don Murphy —if that's your father, he lives over in the next valley now . . ." But he was not listening, his mouth was open and he breathed through it, ran his flat palm up his nose to take care of a drip that had formed there.

"You shacked up with the old fucker, are you? Yeah that'd be right, shack up with some cunt and forget about Samson, to fuck with Samson."

Dog snarled.

"Now then," said Lloyd from behind me, in a teachery voice. I drew myself up to my full height but the man was not put off. He looked at Lloyd.

"An' who the fuck is this bearded prick?" His voice squeaked and he sniffed hard again. The wind knocked him in the back and he stumbled forward a step. There was white spittle at the edges of his mouth. He took a couple of steps back to steady himself and then a couple forward again. Dog's barks rang out over the valley.

"Careful," I said. I heard Lloyd drag Dog to his room to lock him in. The young man looked over my shoulder again.

"Don't put that filthy dog in my bedroom!" he shouted. "What the fuck?" I heard the door close on Dog, and he flung himself against it, howling and scratching. Lloyd came and stood by me.

"Look," said Lloyd, "go over to the next valley and talk to your father. If you don't go away, I'll let the dog out, and he's completely out of control."

I looked at Lloyd.

"Fuck you, grandad." The young man took another step forward, brought his fist up. Lloyd stepped in front of me and pushed him hard in the throat, and the young man gagged and staggered backwards, trying to catch his breath.

"I told you," said Lloyd, "now get lost."

Lloyd had lodged himself in the doorway, suddenly taking up a lot more space than he had before. The boy's face sagged.

"I'm sorry," he whispered and dug his wrists into his eye sockets.

107

"I didn't mean to be rude." He let out a small sob and turned around; in a few paces he was out of sight. From the dark came a muffled cry and the noise echoed around the house long after we'd closed the door. Dog yelped from the bedroom and Lloyd let him out. He turned three circuits of the kitchen table and went to stand by the door, looking at the gap underneath it with dark concentration.

Lloyd clapped his hands together and rubbed them vigorously. "Right," he said loudly, "shall we go to the pub then?"

I'd been to the Blacksmith's Arms a couple of years ago. It hadn't worked out. Sitting at the bar with a pint of something warm and treacly, I'd tried a rocky conversation with the barman.

"The wind always this fierce?" He'd looked at me with an unreadable face.

"Sometimes."

And then a drunk farmer had brushed against me and I'd barked at him. I'd left without drinking even a third of the pint.

When Lloyd went to the bar, I watched how easy it was for him, how the barman volunteered conversation without hesitating. It was warm, the light was low, and rain beat on the windows. Lloyd brought us over whiskies. He'd put too much ice in mine, and I hooked out two cubes and put them in an empty glass. Lloyd watched me but didn't comment. The next one came with just one cube.

"I never come here," I said after a while.

"Why not? It seems nice. Nice ambiance."

I looked at him a while before replying.

"They don't like me."

"Ha!" said Lloyd. I frowned. "They're just interested in you."

"Interested?"

"Christ, I've been here half an hour and two people have already asked how I know you and what sheep you're breeding."

"What did you say?"

"I said I don't, and they're white ones."

I glanced up at the barman, who was looking, and shifted in my seat. Lloyd didn't seem bothered.

"What will you do?" he asked. "About the boy?"

I shrugged. "I'll speak to Don in the morning."

"You think he could be the one—hurting your sheep?"

I turned my glass around on the table a few times. I didn't. Watching him out there against the dark, I'd felt something strange wind its way up around my heart, like I recognised him, like we'd known each other once. Those spittle-grey eyes and desperate mouth.

"I don't know. He seemed mad." I stole a look at Lloyd and then downed my drink. "I'm not that sure it's kids any more. I saw a fox this morning."

"Does he count as a kid?"

I shrugged. "He just seemed batshit."

"Right," said Lloyd.

We watched a teenager try to get served. In his hand he held some keys which I supposed he was hoping looked like the keys to his people carrier or his family townhouse. He wore a badly fitted jacket that on him looked like a school blazer.

"Pint of cider, thanks," he said and the barman didn't move to get the drink, just stared the boy down, resting his hands on the bar in front of him like he was bracing against it. The boy cleared his throat and nodded to the pump. "Cider, pint of, please." He looked like he had considered saying *my good man* at the end, but had rightly decided against it. The barman still did not move, just fixed the boy with a strong look. Then he slowly raised his arm and pointed, without looking, at the sticker underneath the spirits

109

that had an 18 with a red line through it. He didn't say a word, but the boy's ears turned pink. He opened his mouth and closed it and then tried for a leisurely retreat, which he almost carried off, swinging his arms and keeping his knees soft and neck loose. But he stubbed his foot on the rug and it wasn't much of an obstacle, he barely stumbled, but it took the ease out of his departure and the whole face went red and he sped out the door. The barman remained looking at the same spot in front of him like the boy was still there.

"Terrible age," said Lloyd. "Can't do anything with yourself." He drained his drink. "I don't think they had a drinking age when I was a kid. What about you? I bet you got served."

"Why?" I said, sharper than I had meant to.

"I mean, you're tall," he said and looked at his empty glass.

"Drinking laws the same in Australia?" he asked, looking like he'd just thought of a really interesting question, and I realised I'd embarrassed him.

"I guess so," I said. I drained my glass too and went to the bar. The barman looked at me for a moment before coming over.

"Same again?" he asked and I nodded and focused on the bottles on the wall behind him. The transaction took place in silence.

When I got back, Lloyd had found a book on the pub bookshelf called *Teach Yourself: Sheepdog Training*. The photo on the front showed a farmer with thick grey sideburns and his obedient dog sitting at his feet. In the background some Welsh Mountain sheep were penned neatly and cleanly, all looking at the camera.

"It says here," said Lloyd, "that it's possible to teach a collie at any age the basics of sheep control." I put my glass in front of my mouth so that I wouldn't be expected to comment. "Worth a go isn't it?" he asked. I didn't move my glass.

*   *   *

By the time the pub closed, I was too drunk to drive, but Lloyd's eyes were sleepy-looking and he stopped mid-sentence, saying, "Look look look, we can't drive, why don't we—" and either couldn't think of what to say next or forgot he was speaking.

We got in the truck and Dog turned his back on us, disgusted at being left in the car park and at the state we came out of the pub in. I gripped the steering wheel as we left the street lights, and drove deeper into the dark.

"My father told me," said Lloyd in a thick voice, "when I passed my driving test, he said, 'Son, if you're coming home in the car, half-cut, wind down the window and just rest your head on the frame and keep your eyes on the white line at the side of the road. Can't go wrong.'"

I glanced at Lloyd, who had shut his eyes and leant his head back against the headrest. "Can't go wrong," he said again to himself. He was asleep in three minutes, which was good, because I had to concentrate. He snored softly and it made me smile. It was a relief to be heading back with him, that he would be there, downstairs during the night. I hadn't even brought up the idea of driving him into town—it seemed pointless when his bed was already made. There had been a moment not long before closing when he'd got up to get another round and steadied himself on my shoulder as he stood, just for balance. Even though a jolt went through me, like I should stand up and push him over, I hadn't. I'd sat there and while he was at the bar I felt the ghost of his hand on my shoulder and it made me count back to the last time someone had touched me just for balance, just out of absent-minded laziness. I glanced over again at his sleeping profile, the strong bone of his nose, and the truck wobbled a little, so I put my eyes back on the road and squinted into the dark. The headlights lit up a lot of insects for that time of year, white in the beams, large-winged flakes like ash. It took me a while to

111

understand that they weren't insects, that it was snow. I lifted my foot off the accelerator and coasted through the dark watching it fall. I thought to wake Lloyd and show him, but I got the feeling it was performing something just for me. In the headlights a large fox or a deer, but looking nothing like either of those things, ran a split hair in front of the truck and I braked so that Lloyd flew forward and hit his head on the dashboard; there was a squeak from Dog as he rolled off the back seat. "Fuck!" shouted Lloyd.

"Did you see it?" I hissed, yanking on the handbrake and opening the door, forgetting to take off my seatbelt and struggling in the doorway, my breath coming out white.

"See what? I'm bleeding! Jesus Christ. I said we were too drunk to drive."

I stood at the edge of the woods looking hard into the silence, with the snow falling and my heart beating and the engine running. It had looked at me, looked right at me before it disappeared and it was large and dark and its eyes were yellow.

14

Shortland Street is on twice a day and we watch it either in the afternoon or the evening, but sometimes we watch both. There are always drinks that are left on tables, undrunk. Coffee or beer, ordered and then sometimes not even lifted to the lips before the actor storms off, or slopes away with a sad look. Through the whole thing, Otto explains bits to me.

"See that one, he's got a history of playing around—an' that's his ex-wife, but really he's fallen in love with this one over here. But she's after his money." And, "He's referring to the big fire that happened. That's where his father was killed." And I nod and watch the drinks being wasted. By the end I'm thirsty and sad but I think of my last cigarette, hidden where Otto will not look. I've put it on top of my wardrobe and I've been checking on it now and then to make sure nothing has started to eat it or steal the tobacco for a nest. Suddenly though it doesn't matter if a clutch of spiders have made it their home, I'm going to smoke it.

I sneak out to the dunny. I'd thought I'd smoke it in there, but the heat has made the drop toilet even worse than usual, and I think, *Balls to it, I'll just stand behind.* Kelly is under the house panting in the dirt and she doesn't give me a second glance for once, and I feel like a hero lighting the match behind the dunny shed, taking that first deep draw which makes me smile and sends my head into a spin. I don't know how long it's been. Months. Maybe half a year. The smoke gets rid of the flies around my face. A terrorist confidence gets into me and I sneak a look around the corner, and Kelly's back is to me, heaving away under the shadow of the house, and the side wall which faces me has no window, so I come around the front of the shed and stand like anyone else would stand, smoking a cigarette, without anything being the matter, without it being the bad thing to do and without the slightest worry. Underneath the house the dirt is lumpy from Kelly's digging. I've seen her before dragging some animal's stinking carcass out of the paddock and starting to bury it there. If she catches me looking she stops, out-stares me and waits for me to leave so she can dig in secrecy. Like she's stocking a larder.

The sun is at that moment not an unbearable sting on my eyes, but a clean memory of being a kid, and of having got one over the olds. I close my eyes and think of the smell of eucalypt in the heat. It could be the hit from the cigarette, but I feel good. I open my eyes because there's a noise, and I hold the smoke I've sucked in deep in my lungs. Otto has come out of the house and is unbuttoning himself at the veranda. He is facing me, there's no way he can't see me, but he doesn't. Don't move, *The human eye senses movement before all else.* I don't move, I don't blink or exhale, and Otto pisses a long stretch of yellow out over the veranda. It lands not too far from where Kelly is lying heaving in the dirt, and she whips her head around and looks at the mud puddle it makes on the ground, ears up. I can see that between her paws is a woman's shoe, hot pink and to fit a very small foot. She has chewed the heel off it, the toe is sharp and pointed. Kelly is unimpressed by the urine and goes back to staring into the dark. Otto cracks off a fart and sighs. My hand trembles but I still it. He shakes his little cock off once, twice, then stuffs it back in his pants, singing a song of his own invention which goes *Doodle dee doodle doo*, as he turns around and walks back into the house, the fly-screen smashing behind him.

*   *   *

114

Otto's in a good mood today and so I get a driving lesson—my first in months. It all comes together much more easily. I'm smoother, and Otto shows me how to reverse, and it gives me no problems at all. I get up a bit of speed, and the air comes in sweet through the window. Otto chuckles less this time, and when we get back to the house his mood's changed. Quiet, like there's something on his mind.

"You okay, baby?" I ask him, hanging my arms around his shoulders. I want to be good so that he lets me drive more. His face darkens a little.

"Don't use that slut talk with me," he says and moves my arms away so they fall at my sides. He can get cranky when he's hungry, so I fix him some sandwiches made with cold lamb and yellow mustard. He eats them but doesn't look at me, instead he's looking out at the truck while he licks his fingers.

A couple of days pass and when I ask him about having another go, he laughs. "Why do you need to learn? You want to take Kelly on a date?" He laughs so much at this that by the end I have trouble holding my smile. I don't ask again for a couple of days until I've thought up a reason.

"What if something happens to you? All the way out here, I'd need to get you to a doctor."

He is annoyed, and he waves me away. "I'm not going in any bloody hospital," he says and that's that. I don't ask what would happen to me, left here with Kelly, if I couldn't drive myself out—left like those sheep after Carole had gone.

I shear the sheep alone in the following days. By the third day I'm getting fast at it, the flies don't bother me any more. I slow down because once they're shorn there will be no excuse to be out here all day. I take breaks in between each sheep and dig antlions out of their holes with a stalk of grass, watching them attack it and then burrow away backwards. I find a horned lizard that thinks I can't see it, watch it shift standing feet like a dancer, and the paper skin of a brown snake. There is always a large bird passing overhead, looking at the sheep or a rabbit, or the lizard or me.

I make the final ten last me a whole day, and then I consider going back over the first ones, the ones I did when I was less sure of myself, but even those are not bad.

Karen is in the supermarket. I cannot believe it. She's comparing two packets of cereal bars, and her eyes go large and round when she sees me, but she smiles too. I go to hug her, but she holds up her hand between us to show me the sparkly ring on her finger and says in the same breath, "I've got meself married, what are you doing here?" And I take a second to see what she means; a bloke with a hat pulled low over his face has looked up at us from the newspaper stand, and she nods to him.

"Oh, I'm staying with my uncle," I say in a way I hope she will get what I mean. I point to Otto who is waiting outside the shop, watching and looking uncomfortable.

"That's great," says Karen and she's still smiling, but just with her lips. She looks frightened, if I let myself think about it.

"Where are you living?" I ask her, and her eyes dart over my face and her smile fades.

"Stay safe, darl," she whispers and hands me her box of cereal bars, and as she does it she strokes the back of my hand, hidden behind the box. She turns and walks down the aisle to the guy in the hat who is watching with a frown on his face. She takes him by the elbow and laughs high and flirty and mumbles something to him. He takes one more look at me and pulls his hat down and they leave the shop without buying anything; Karen glances back once and then is lost, and I am not sure any more if I actually saw her, if she was really there or if I imagined it. I pretend I am also interested in the cereal bars, I pick up one that has chocolate on one side and one that is made with real honey and hold them out next to each other in front of me. There is a yank on my heart, which takes me a little bit to still. I'd like to be able to have a Coke with Karen. I remember the air at the harbour and wonder if life was so bad back then after all.

In the truck, Otto says, "Who was that?"

"Just an old friend," I tell him, and when he looks sharp I say, "More of an *acquaintance*." He doesn't talk all the way back to the station, which is fine by me, because I'm thinking of all those times with a six-pack down by the beach when me and Karen'd take a night off, even if we couldn't afford it. I think about when she gave me five whole packets of Holidays because a regular had gone abroad and got her duty-free. I hope the bloke with the hat is good, I hope he is the one that got her the duty-free.

That night, I hear Otto padding down the hall to my room, and I start to make myself ready. He likes to be able to see my scars these days, says it makes him feel protective over me which I guess can't be a bad thing. So I yank up my T-shirt over my head, and I've hooked my thumbs into the sides of my shorts to pull them off too, but his footsteps stop outside my door, and he doesn't come in. Instead there's a scraping noise, and the doorknob rattles. Still he doesn't come in and I'm looking at the door expecting him to walk through it, but then his footsteps go back down the hallway, and I realise he has locked the door to my room.

Right, I think.

A fortnight later, I am cleaning the oven when Otto comes into the kitchen holding his hat in his hands.

"I'm going to the shops," he says, turning the hat around a full circle. I get up from the floor and pull the handkerchief from my head.

"I'll just wash my hands, then I'll be ready," I say, but Otto lets go of the hat with one hand and holds his palm down to the floor.

"No—you stay here," he says. "I can see you're busy."

"It's fine, I can leave the oven-cleaner to work—I need some more Dettol for the sheep—the flies—"

Otto interrupts to say, "I'll get that for you."

I go to the sink anyway to wash my hands, hang the rubber gloves over the faucet. "It's fine, I can finish the oven later."

My back is turned to him and he says in a voice with an edge to it, "You'll stay here." And the fly-screen snaps behind him.

When I turn around, he is getting into the truck and leaving Kelly, which he never does. Kelly stands out the front watching him leave, and then she turns to look at me. I put my hand up to the fly-screen and she lowers her head, keeps her eyes trained on me. I'm not to leave the house.

When he gets back that evening, I see Otto take out the keys, and I see him lock the ute up and hang the keys high up above the sink. He's never locked the ute before. Not even in town. I take this small thing that I see to bed and think about it as I watch out the window. There has been a change—I can sense it in the smell of the place, which has started to get to me.

And when he comes to my room, the sex is different, it's too tender, makes me feel like I'm made of wax. He holds my trunk for a long time afterwards, his head resting on my belly. He kisses the space above my navel and sighs into me. I look at the bald spot at the top of his head that is covered in liver spots, and where the hair is greased by his own scalp. I get the feeling

118

I'd rather be fucked hard and hated, I'd rather his socks in my mouth.

"Do you need anything?" he asks me. "Do you need the loo?"

When I come back from the toilet he has smoothed over my bed sheets and put a glass of water on the table by the bed. He pulls back the sheets for me to get in, and when I comply, he tugs up the sheets around my shoulders, makes sure my man's arms are covered, even though it's a hot night. He tucks my feet in so that my toes point downwards. He kisses my forehead and tells me, "Goodnight, sleep tight." And in that moment I think I might cry, but I manage to wait until he has left the room and I hear the click of him locking me in again. Kelly scratches in the dirt underneath the house and tonight I cannot bear the sound. I get out of bed and hit the metal cage of my window to try and get her to go away. She barks loudly and I sit back down on my bed and wait to hear Otto's footsteps padding down past my room and looking out on Kelly. I hear him say, "What's it?" and Kelly's whine. "Good girl," he says quietly and he goes back to bed, pausing at my door, listening perhaps. I bounce a little on the bed, to make a noise like I might be turning over in my sleep. I hear Kelly growl, then bite at the fleas on her back. She heaves herself up and starts to dig again. I get quietly out of bed and I do push-ups in the dark. When my arms can't take my weight any more, I do sit-ups and finally I crawl into bed and as I fall asleep a bird cries in the night, and it sounds just like a fire horn.

15

The next morning when the wind had stopped blowing, the mist came down thicker than I'd seen before. It lapped at my feet when I opened the door, like my house was an island. Dog strode off into it, and lost his legs and hovered smoothly. In the woolshed I dug out the unopened fox bait that had been there since I moved in. I put it in my pocket and thought about how probably I wouldn't lay it, but it was good to feel like I could if I wanted to. I doubted it would do anything much to an animal the size of the one I'd seen on the way home. I tried to remember the shape of the thing, but all I had left in my memory was a set of yellow eyes.

Outside Lloyd was shaking his finger at Dog. I started when he yelled, "No!"

Dog sat at Lloyd's feet, with his ears back and one foot raised. He looked pissed off.

"What's going on?"

Lloyd ignored me and said Dog's name in a creepy way. He was saying it the way people talk to a baby, with too many ups and downs so it sounded like "Doo-erg," and looking Dog right in the eye at the same time. The hackles on Dog's shoulders were up more every time Lloyd said it, until Dog couldn't take it any more and barked his warning bark, the high-pitched one that meant *Get lost*. As soon as he'd barked, Lloyd yelled "NO!" in a deep voice and Dog cowered down, but his ears flicked about and he looked ready to murder.

"What the hell are you doing?" I asked.

When Lloyd looked up, Dog started to slink away up the field.

"The book says you need to get him to know his name." He bent down and picked up the book lying on the ground which he'd taken with him from the pub. I hoped nobody had seen. He read out, in a booming voice, "'Your puppy should learn his name right away. Say his name often in a gentle voice.'"

"Dog is four years old, and he knows he's Dog already," I said. "You're just pissing him off. He'll bite you."

Lloyd carried on, "'It is imperative you teach your dog *not* to bark when working. Yell NO! at him harshly. If he does not listen, grab him by the nose and say NO! firmly.'"

"He is going to bite you," I said again.

Lloyd waved his hand at me. "We have an understanding now," he said and looked around for Dog, who was still trying to make his way inside without being noticed. "Here!" Lloyd shouted sternly, pointing to his feet, and fair do, Dog shuffled back to him. "See!" said Lloyd, resting his weight on a crook and looking very pleased with himself. "He knows who's boss."

I went back inside, put on a pot of coffee and watched from the kitchen window. Lloyd started up with his gooey naming again and Dog barked, three times, so Lloyd shouted NO! NO! NO! one for each bark.

Dog's ears were flat to his head, and he put his bum up in the air, his chin down low. "Doo-erg," said Lloyd, pointing at him. Dog made six high-pitched yips, wiggled his arse and lunged at Lloyd's face. After impact, Dog seemed free of rage, and trotted happily back towards the house, his work completed.

Lloyd was bent over, cupping his nose in his hand. He checked for blood and there must have been some because then he threw his crook away from him and stamped his foot like a toddler. I let Dog in and gave him a biscuit.

121

When Lloyd came in he had his scarf wrapped around his face and neither of us mentioned it. He glanced at Dog and Dog pretended not to see him.

"I'm going to check on the sheep," I said, looking at the space near his head.

"Great," he said, maybe a bit too brightly, "I'll come too."

"I did warn you, and to be fair, so did Dog."

Lloyd poured himself some coffee. He took his scarf off to drink.

"It was more of a head-butt than a bite," he said.

I nodded, taking in his red nose. "He must like you."

Lloyd squinted at me like he was trying to work out if I was taking the piss, and I tried to look serious.

On our way out the door, Dog caught a mouse and tossed it about while it squeaked, keeping it alive for too long. Eventually though, he crunched it up. Lloyd avoided looking at him.

"Sometimes I don't know you at all," I said to Dog, but he wasn't bothered.

We walked in silence up the steep way to the top field. Lloyd wheezed behind me. When I looked there was a soft frown on his face and he leant heavily on his stick. I stopped and pretended to check the fence. Lloyd panted.

"What are those for?" he asked, pointing at some dried moles that hung from the fence. Don's work.

"Telling the time," I said.

"Really?" He bent down and squinted at the closest mole, as flat and dry as the sole of a shoe. "Is it like a sundial?"

I looked at him to see if he was joking. He switched eyes.

"They make the ground lumpy," I said, but he either misunderstood or didn't understand anything at all because he continued to squint at the mole from different angles. We moved on up the hill towards the top field, and I picked an old sloe and handed it to Lloyd.

122

"You can eat these," I said, and he bit into it.

"Fuck," he said, and spat it out.

I laughed. "Have you not seen *Crocodile Dundee*?"

Lloyd wiped his mouth over and over on the back of his hand. "Stop picking on me," he said.

At the top of the hill, I shook a can of feed and watched the faces bob up and scrutinise me. A few of the greedier and more pregnant ewes started forward, their bellies swaying like hammocks.

"I need to move some of them into the shed," I said. "Could use your help." Usually one or two went their own way when I tried mustering them down to the pens, and it took a while on my own to get them back.

Lloyd looked steadily at the sheep approaching and said nothing. He looked like he was thinking about running away. I tied Dog to the fence so he wouldn't interfere.

"You stand there," I said, pointing to a spot just beyond the gate, "and stop them from escaping." I opened the gate to the top field. "Wave your hands about if they run for you. Shout at them. That sort of thing."

"What do I shout?"

I looked at him.

"Whatever you like."

I rattled the shaker again and a few more lifted their heads up and stared. Some began bustling down towards us, others followed.

"Here sheep sheep sheep," I called.

As they got closer, I backed away, so that they would follow me into the other field. The first fifteen or so were in the bottom field, and then a Blueface with twins inside her gave the eye to Lloyd. He saw her coming and sent his legs wide apart and waved his arms about. The sheep kept on going, and Lloyd yelled, "Fuck you!" at the sheep, which peeled off away from him and back down the hill. Dog whipped around on the end of his rope like a pike eel.

I closed the gate and gave them what was in the shaker.

Lloyd untied Dog, who peed angrily against the gate post then patrolled up and down, his hair raised. Lloyd leant heavily on the fence.

"You okay?" I asked and he straightened up. I tried not to smile.

"It was all I could think to shout."

I shrugged. "Worked."

Lloyd wiped his mouth on the back of his hand. His eyes brightened.

"Quite invigorating really," he said.

I walked up to the hawthorn stile and looked back down on the house. Over on Don's side of the hill I could see the yellow glow of his electric lights—every window lit, even in daylight, like he was trying to burn off the fog with them. On the border of his property, I saw the vixen again, dragging with her a large bird, a pheasant maybe, I was too far away to tell. She pranced, holding her kill high, weaving and bouncing. I glanced at Dog but he had his nose to the ground smelling out the things that had been there in the dark. If her cubs had made it, they'd be getting bigger soon, hungrier, and the lambs were coming. I watched her disappear into the woods, and heard on the air the far-away tinkle of Don's digital radio, which played tinny pop music. I patted the pocket with the fox bait in.

"Hey." A girl was sitting on the stile, smoking. "You're the woman in Samson's old house."

"Who are you?" I said, suddenly aware that I may have been talking out loud to myself.

The girl blew out a waterfall of smoke which played over her face. It must've stung her eyes but she showed no sign of that.

"I'm Marcie. I went to the same school as him. I know you from the shop."

"Oh." She looked different out of her thick green tracksuit. She wore a full face of make-up and her hair was dirty blond, straight and still.

Marcie narrowed her eyes at me. "This is public property, you can't do anything about me being here." She squinted at me.

"No. Would be good if you took your rubbish with you though." She didn't react, apart from to take an open can of drink from the pocket of her overcoat. She drank it looking me in the eye, like she was waiting for me to be shocked.

"What are you doing anyway?" she asked, putting her can carefully back in her pocket.

"I'm laying fox bait," I said, to have something definite and grown-up to offer her.

"Isn't that against the law?"

"That's fox hunting."

"Same difference."

"Not how most people see it."

She lifted herself off the stile and came and stood next to me. Dog presented his nose to her and she touched it.

"Your dog's pretty wild-looking."

"He's okay."

"What's his name?"

I toyed with making one up to avoid the questions, but couldn't think of a name that would be convincing.

"Dog."

Marcie shrugged off this information.

"So what've you got against the foxes?"

"It's lambing season. You'd know that, being from around here?"

She hissed breath through her teeth. "I keep out of it. As soon as I can I'm away from here anyway." She drew her hair back from her head into a high ponytail and held it there. "I want to be in London. Or Sheffield."

"Cities can be crappy places too," I said.

She shrugged and let her hair drop back down to her shoulders. "At least they're not boring."

"I suppose."

"So they eat the lambs?"

"What?"

"The foxes?"

"Yes. I've seen you before."

Marcie's face showed no surprise or intrigue. "I told you—I know you from the shop. Anyway, everyone here has seen everyone before."

"Out on the Military Road. I've seen you there before. Your friend showed me his arse."

"He shows everyone."

"It wasn't very nice."

"Take it up with him," she said and got her cigarettes out of her pocket. She shook two out. "Smoke?"

I looked at her for a moment. "Thanks." I don't know if she expected me to take one, but again, there was no reaction. She held a lighter out to me and I made a shield with my hands to light up then handed it back.

"You're younger than everyone else," she said.

"How do you mean?"

"Everyone else who has a farm. And you're a woman."

"I am," I said, and blew out smoke. For the first time she raised her eyebrows, but she closed her eyes as she did it which perhaps meant it was not surprise but something else. Disgust maybe.

"Is that man you're hanging out with your boyfriend?"

I frowned. "Have you been watching me?"

126

She shrugged again.

"He's just passing through. I don't really know him."

"You just let people you don't know stay in your house? Well, I suppose it keeps it fresh. You know he's been doing some pretty funny shit around the place."

"What kind of funny shit?"

She shrugged again. "Sings to your dog quite a lot."

We both looked at Dog, who gave a slow wag of his tail then looked away up the hill like he was thinking of something else.

"He's a strange man," I said.

Marcie smiled, and I smiled back. I would have liked her if I was her age.

"Shouldn't you be in school?"

She behaved as if she hadn't heard me. "So this vendetta against the foxes—how come there are so many about if you lay all this poison for them?"

"I don't usually."

"So why now?"

"Something's been killing my sheep."

"Has it?"

"It has. In fact, I thought it might have something to do with your lot."

Marcie's eyes widened but again she didn't really address what I said. "I have this cousin, Wesley, on my mum's side—he's on the mainland but up north, way up north—and he's just got in trouble for messing with horses."

"What kind of messing?"

"What—do I have to spell it out for you? He fucked a horse," she said and there was silence. Then Marcie giggled and I smiled.

"Don't worry about spelling it out for me in the future," I said.

She took her can out of her pocket and took a swig. It was

127

super-strength lager. After a pause she offered it to me. I shook my head.

"Aren't you young to drink?"

She cocked her head to the side. "Something?"

"Huh?"

"You didn't say foxes are killing your sheep—you said something is killing your sheep. So you don't really think it's foxes?"

"I don't know." I used the cigarette to pause the conversation. I blew smoke out and it disappeared against the white sky. "Do you ever see . . . anything?" I said. "I mean it feels like you're out there all the time."

Marcie smiled. "We see everything," she said, like she thought she was a teen witch. "I've seen things you couldn't imagine." She looked into the distance and her smile softened a little. "But mostly, it's just people having sex with each other."

"Anything that might be killing my sheep? Anybody?"

"Oh!" she said loudly. "There was a big fuck-off bear or some shit that Samson was telling us about."

"A bear?"

"Not a bear—a big cat or a big dog or something. A beast. Samson's full of shit though. He's a bit . . . retarded, if that's allowed. Mentally challenged? I don't know. It's not as bad as when my dad calls them coloureds."

"What did he say?"

"He said he doesn't want any coloured people moving into the lane, not because he's racist but because it'll mean the house is worth less."

"What did Samson say, about the beast?"

"Oh, I don't know—it might have just had big feet or teeth or something. I think he's telling stories. He likes telling stories. Sometimes he camps in the woods, and he reckons something was

128

licking his tent in the night, that he shone his torch on it and it was this cat-eyed thing. I told him, it's just the weed." She glanced at me when she said "weed."

We watched rain start across the valley. Marcie dropped her cigarette on the ground and pressed it into the mud with her heel.

16

We drive through an old flaky wooden gate and up to a homestead. I turn to look in all directions, but there is nothing to see—some black hills long and far in the distance, a backdrop for the desert. I can see flies in the air, and my window-side arm is sunburnt.

"Well, here we are then!" Otto says brightly, and I can tell he's excited to show me the place. An old dog, far older than the photograph he showed me from his wallet, lumbers up to us.

"This must be Kelly?" I say in a voice I reckon a dog would like. The dog looks at me blankly through clouded eyes. She's got a grey muzzle and patches of dry skin show through on her flank. *Poor old thing*, I think.

"Kelly, meet Jake," says Otto, and I squat down to make friends, but she keeps her distance. Just gives me that look like I'm not there, and turns and heads back behind the house, her ears flat to her head against the flies. "She gets cranky when I leave without her," he explains.

I get a small tour. "Like I said, we're pretty much self-sufficient here," says Otto, and I wonder if there's a greener patch around the back for vegetables. There is a hairy-looking paddock next to the house, but it's dry and wild. "We slaughter our own sheep, and so really it's just basics we shop for, twice a month or so. Bread, eggs and beer. I've tried a few chickens, but they don't last long—Kelly doesn't take to them too well." I wonder if "we" means there's someone else around the place or if he just means his dog. There is no green space around the back, there's just the dunny and then beyond that, the rest of everything. The watering hole has dried up because of the drought, he tells me, and it doesn't seem right to say anything more on the subject. The house is made of splintery weatherboard. It's small, the kind you see carted up and down highways on the back of road trains.

Otto shows me into a bedroom. It's an odd room, there's a Winnie the Pooh poster on the wall and the narrow single bed's doona has a faded pony on it. The room is painted pale blancmange and there's a smallish window with no glass but with mosquito netting nailed over it. It smells of air freshener.

"Did it up meself," Otto says with pride.

I start to get twitchy once the sun goes down. Otto makes bacon sandwiches for tea, which smell and taste of other meats. I don't know what the plan is, what he's expecting from me. "You like *Shortland Street*?" he says as he pats the sofa next to him. I sit down and he puts a hand around the back of my neck so that I can smell the undercarriage of his arm.

"Never seen it," I say, and he looks at me like I'm telling him I've never seen the sea. The theme tune comes on, and Otto looks at me with meaning as he sings it.

> Is it you or is it me?
> Lately I've been lost it seems.
> I think a change is what I need.
> If I'm looking for a chance I've a dream.
> Shortland Street . . .

His eyes mist over and he holds the last note long enough that the television has gotten well into the second verse before he's

131

finished. He shakes his head. "That's just beautiful," he says, "that song. Just beautiful." And for the next half-hour we watch comings and goings at a hospital. Kelly is sitting outside looking through the fly-screen at me.

Once the programme is over, Otto stretches and says, "Right-e-o, time for bed," and I think, *Here we go, this'll make things clearer.* He leads me into the pink room and sits on the edge of the bed chatting about what we'll do tomorrow.

"I'll take you into town so you can get acquainted with the general store, then we'll go and show you the sheep. Kelly needs some tick drops, so remind me about those." I don't know what the protocol is, so I change into the T-shirt I sleep in while he's talking. I don't turn my back to him when I take my top off but he just carries on, and so I sit next to him on the bed and he tells me about his sheep. "The ex-wife's show sheep—merinos, she insisted on, even though I told her, too dry out here, they take looking after. She went on and on, and then once I got them for her she lost interest. Expensive buggers they are too. And then, well, she went, and so I just use them for meat. I told her, right off the bat, those sorta sheep are no good out here where there's no grass—need a desert sheep, something tough and wiry. She wouldn't listen though, just like with her poofy little dog she brought along. Me and Kelly were clear to her about that dog, we warned her. No good with your peking-fuckin-eses, a farm. Carpet snake I reckon, took it under the house, probably swallowed the nut whole."

He laughs and his stomach shakes. I smile at him, hoping it's a joke, and slide under the sheets, which are crinkly and new. Otto stalls in his chat and looks at me. He sighs and wipes his large old hand over my cheek. "Jeeze," he says, "I always wanted a daughter." He smiles and his eyes are filling, and he raises a finger to his eyelashes before pulling himself together. "Wait there a second," he says, and disappears out of the room. When he comes back he is carrying a plush brown bear holding a velvet heart, and a disposable camera. "For you," he says, with that same soppy look about him. I take the bear and I smile.

"Thanks, he's really nice," I say and sit the bear on my lap. Otto walks back a few feet and aims the camera at me. I smile, hug the bear. He uses up all the film in his camera just on me and that bear.

"Sweet dreams then, pet," he says and I get a kiss on the forehead. I smile back at him and he sighs again from the doorway, looking back at me with those wet eyes before he turns out the light and closes the door. The window throws a chequered light on the Winnie the Pooh poster.

In the morning, because the land is so flat, I can see that the sheep, far off in the distance, are penned.

"You can have the use of the push-bike till you learn to drive—there's a spare truck in the shed I've been fixing up and that'll be yours once you know how." Otto pinches my arm like he's a fun uncle. I smile at the idea of it—owning a truck. I could pick Karen up and bring her for a visit, once the waterhole fills again.

We drive off to meet the sheep. As we get closer I can see how ill they look—patches of wool missing, ribs poking out. There's a smell of shit and you can see the maggots eating their hind-quarters. Man up, I tell myself, he's an old bloke, he's doing the best he can.

The flies are fierce, they try and get at the wet in our eyes, and I breathe through my teeth in case I suck one in.

Otto shows me out in the pen how to catch one and keep her down, and I can see he's pleased when I manage to grab hold of one and flip her onto her back without too much of a problem.

I can feel her heartbeat through me, and she smells bad. Otto stands with his hands on his hips.

"Knew I'd chosen a goodun, by the size of you," he says and slaps me on the thigh.

Otto keeps the sheep penned next to the woolshed which, he shows me, is also at times a slaughterhouse. "Can't let them just roam off when it's me on my own out here," he says. "Don't like to get strangers in here to shear—that's when things started to go bad with Carole." There's an uncomfortable pause, and I look at the old blood that has turned dry and black on the floor under the meat hook. The place smells of stale vomit and bleach. "An' this way they don't know if they're getting a hair cut or if they're getting their throats cut, so really it's calming?" I try to look like I agree with him.

In the kitchen I make a pretty terrible mess, the air thick with smoke from the fat off the chops. Once it's done, Otto shovels in what I've made him, says he loves it, even though I could only work out how to scramble the eggs, and they are crumbly and the pot I cook them in needs to soak for three days before the burn comes off it. The sausages are pink in the middle, and the chops are fatty, surprising when you look at the type of sheep they came from. I pick at my food but Otto eats all of his.

That night, he comes for me while I'm in the shower, and I panic. I always managed to keep on my T-shirt before. He gets in with me, his hairless belly grazing me and his cock hangs in that in-between state like the end of it is attached to a thread. I try and keep him occupied with my boobs; I wiggle them about, but he's less interested than I'd have hoped—I have never been the kind of girl who is about the boobs. He wants to scrub my back, and do all the kind of things I suppose you'd want to do in the event of caring about someone. I think I would rather a sharp jab in the back of the throat, because as he puts his arms around me and slides his hands over my ribs and along my spine, his breath catches and his fingers stop on the ridges on my back. He doesn't say anything, and I don't stop him as he turns me around to look. He traces the scars with his fingertips, and he says, "My god, my god," as he does it. "Why didn't I know about this?" And I wonder if he'll dump me back in Port Hedland and find another less ruined girl to cook his chops and share his showers.

"Was it a customer?" he asks and I nod, letting the lie set immediately. I make it the man with the bleach-blond hair and shaved balls who wanted to put his dirty socks in my mouth. He came in my face and on his socks. Then he took the socks out of my mouth and he put them on his feet and put his feet in his sandals and trotted off home. I made it him, but instead of socks he'd undone his buckled belt—in reality he was the sort that didn't wear a belt and preferred everyone to be able to see the top bristles of his shaved bits. I tell this story to Otto as he sits on the toilet seat with a yellow towel wrapped around him and I lean against the sink, feeling how loose it is from the wall.

Otto wipes tears from his eyes. "You girls," he says, "what a time of it you have." And he gestures that I should come and lay my head in his lap, kneel on the toilet mat, and he sobs over me as I race through the details of my lie in my head, file it away in my memory and close the door on it. Slowly Otto moves aside his yellow towel and that's how I end up giving him head while he's sat on the toilet.

Around the house is a paddock of tall strange grasses. They are strange because of the things hidden in them that poke out into the air—push-bikes without wheels, farm tools that are the colour of earth from rust. Every now and then if you pass the paddock

135

on your way to the dunny, you spy a sheep's skull among the tin cans and broken chainsaws. Sometimes it's like there's a tiger out there, like it can see me but I can't see it. If I stand looking for too long, Kelly is liable to stand up and ask, *What are you loitering for, and don't test me to see if I'll bark.*

Kelly doesn't like me. She's not like a dog really; she's more disapproving than a dog. She sees things differently to the way most dogs do—she's not into pats on the head, she won't take food from my hand. I offer her the meat from my sandwich one time and she stands, looking through me until I feel embarrassed and put it back in the bread. Another time I absent-mindedly bend down to scratch behind her ear while Otto is telling me how he likes his home kept, and she snaps at my hand, breaks the skin on my little finger. Otto frowns. "She doesn't like that," he says. She watches me in a way I recognise, but not from a dog.

I have not seen a phone in the house, and I ask Otto about it.

"Phone?" he says. "Who would we call? The Ghostbusters?" He laughs. This is a thing I'm learning about him—he likes to laugh at his jokes.

Somewhere into the fifth week, Otto has only called for sex a dozen or so times. He's just a kind, lonely old man. He only ever wants it in a normal way. He drives us into town to get supplies, to the store which has everything—food and hardware and furniture and animal feed and rat poison and grog. My palms sweat. Otto has given me $100 for groceries, which is more than I know what to do with. I pick up a can of cream, the same kind that Mum used to squirt onto her daiquiris. She called it a grog float. I put the can down carefully and turn away from it. I remember what Otto said about Carole's cooking, and I find eggs and bread, some cheese. Otto does not have a deep-fat fryer, so I do not put the great sacks of frozen chips or, though I eye them, the

136

ready-dipped calamari rings in the trolley. As a gift, he buys me a pink shampoo with a picture of a horse on it. At the checkout, I go to give him a peck on the cheek, and he stiffens. "You're my niece," he says, "remember that." And I glance over at the checkout lady who looks quickly down at her till.

I wonder how those sheep are still alive, how long they've been trapped there next to their slaughterhouse. Since Carole left? I don't know how long that has been.

The pen is made up of flimsy metal barriers that can be linked or separated and moved one at a time. The sections are not heavy and the sheep, if they had a mind to, could probably break out, but they don't do a lot of anything much, just shift their weight from their hips to their shoulders and stare out at the horizon while the flies eat their backsides.

The earth in their enclosure is coated in shit and just a few feet to the left of their pen is a dusting, at least, of grass. I start to shift the pen, panel by panel, expanding it slightly, edging the sheep over towards the grass. When they get in my way, I herd and shoo them, waving my arms. They are not bothered enough to be scared, but they more or less go where I tell them. They move with the weight of ghosts and I notice a few are resting on the front joints of their legs, like they haven't got the strength to stand. It takes me two hours, during which time Otto and Kelly drive up to see why I've been gone so long.

Otto frowns at first, but then he shrugs. "Might get some meat on them I suppose," and he drives back to the house while Kelly watches out of the back of the ute.

The flies drink out of the corners of my eyes, and crawl all over my shoulders, and I let them crawl. I'm not sure what I was expecting, to see the sheep dance gratefully around in the puny grass I've found them, but they just stand there, a silent little group. I try to move them about, but they're not scared of me. Resigned is what they are, and I tell them, "You can move around if you want to," waving my arms and jumping about, but they just sway a little in the hot fly air. I look at the woolshed and see the meat hook and I shift onto my other foot. "Fair enough," I say and cycle back to the house, and put the sheep far in the back crevice of my mind, with those other things that only come out in the dark when my guard is down and I stare at the night behind my window cage.

There's a black-and-white photograph on the wall in the telly room and Otto sees me looking at it. It's him with dark hair and a trim waist, and he's holding some kind of trophy.

"Golden Shears, 1962," he says. He's standing with a woman who wears high-waisted trousers and an old-fashioned hairdo and who is presenting him with the trophy, a pair of scissors soldered onto a plinth. "That's Candy Mulligan—she was the weather girl from ABC. She had a thing for me."

I look at the man in the picture with the sun-crinkled face and the straight back. Dark hair feathering out from under his hat.

He turns up the volume on the TV. "Ah—it's me programme," he says.

Otto gives me a lesson in driving. He takes me out where there's nothing to smash into and lets me turn slow doughnuts in the dust. When we stall and when I make the truck rattle with going too slow, he laughs at me, but I've never felt so capable, and I think about when the other truck is fixed and when I can take off down the dirt road and out onto the bitumen. If you have wheels, I realise, you are free.

After the lesson, Otto shows me what he's doing to the other truck. The bonnet is up and inside is another language of tubes and cables.

"See this?" he says, slapping a black box with the flat of his hand. "Couple of loose connections in there I reckon, nothing major." He blushes a little and looks away. "I wanted to have her ready for when you arrived, but me flamin' hands went crook." I put my hand on Otto's shoulder and smile at him.

Late in the day, I'm standing out on the veranda smoking a Holiday and Kelly is standing on all fours barking at me like she really wants to go for me. Otto comes out looking uncomfortable.

"No smoking here, pet, upsets the dog. Reminds her of Carole— she and Carole didn't get along," he says and I exhale and look at the tip of my cigarette. I feel awkward and embarrassed, like a kid again.

"Okay," I say, "last one." It's fine, I think, I'll just have to do it when I'm on my own, but he comes and takes the cigarette out of my fingers and drops it cherry first into his mug of tea. Then he holds out his hand.

"And the rest."

"That was my last," I say, counting up the packets I have left from the duty-free Karen gave me. I think there are two and a half-finished pack, but as long as I can find fifty cents here and there, I'll be able to sneak a packet now and again, it's not such a hardship.

"Hm," says Otto, frowning. "Bad for a person's health."

Otto has a beer early and falls asleep in front of the afternoon soaps—he can watch them again in the evening runs, so it's not a drama. Because the house is so hot, I leave a note and climb on my bike. Kelly lifts her head at me as I cycle off up the track to the sheep, but she doesn't bark and wake Otto.

I fill their trough with fresh water and scatter some pellets around the place. They aren't that interested and who could blame them. There's almost no shade, and the ones with the paler faces must be blistering with skin cancers. Mostly, they crowd along the wall of the shed where the roof shelters them a little from the sun. The flies are swarming again, clouds of them, they muscle in at the sheep's eyes and arseholes. I try spraying the sheep with the hose, but I can't tell if it helps or if they like it, they just hang there on their feet. If I could get hold of a couple of lengths of wood, I could hang over a tarpaulin and give them a little shade. The man with the black hair in the photo on Otto's wall wouldn't object to that. Maybe it was just his crook hands that stopped him from looking after the sheep, maybe he just needs the extra help. I get on my bike and ride back to the house, slowly, thinking.

Inside, my last packets of Holidays are laid out on the front table.

"Now, I'm not cross," says Otto, "because I know this is an addiction. But what we're doing here today is we're taking a stand against it."

I stop myself just short of raising my voice when I say, "You went through my things?"

"Your things, young lady, are in my house." He says it with an edge of hardness like he thinks he's my dad, and it makes my heart beat fast. I think I will cry.

"Come and stand next to me, pet," he says.

Kelly is sitting bolt upright in the dirt, waiting for something. Otto picks up the first packet and lobs it off the veranda to her. The dog pounces on it like it's alive, snarling and growling, the flesh of the inside of her mouth showing, saliva greasing all over the cardboard.

She wrecks them, shaking the packet, slinging cigarettes

140

everywhere, rolling on them once they're out. And Otto throws the next packet. Kelly does not lose focus.

"Now," says Otto, once it is all done and I am standing in silence next to him, gripping the wood of the veranda. He hands me a dustpan and brush. "You go and clean all that mess up and put it in the bin and we'll say no more about it."

Kelly does not growl at me while I sweep it up but she watches me and I'd like to kick her hard in the ribs.

I go to my room and sit on the edge of the bed with a feeling I can't be exact about spinning round in my stomach. I look at my bag, which I hadn't thought to unpack since I arrived.

Otto is bright and chirpy, and we have a busy day because it's time to teach me to shear.

"Bin thinking," he says, "about what you done with the pen, and giving the sheep a bit more space—p'raps it's good for 'em—don't seem so maggoty any more. If we could get those girls in a more acceptable state, might be a few we could mate, and we could get things going again. Arse has dropped out of wool, but maybe if we could get the meat sellable," he says, full of himself, chirruping away. I am tired and he looks hurt.

In the woolshed, he hands me some shears which don't look far different from the ones Mum used to use on the triplets' hair. He shows me how to work them, and Kelly sniffs round the place, in particular at the black stains underneath the meat hook.

"Get yourself a sheep then." I look at him a bit blankly. "G'wan," he says, "you're not shearing me!" which he thinks is a hilarious joke and he doubles over laughing. I go and get hold of a sheep around the hips. She doesn't struggle, but isn't wanting to move, and it's difficult persuading her up the ramp to the shed. She might be wondering which bit of her is getting cut, but I get her up there, and Otto shows me how to position her to start. When he has her pinned on the boards, a strange gentleness comes over him, I can see it in his face. It's like how he looks at me when we screw.

"You don't want her to be sitting on her tail," he says, "cause that's not comfortable," and he demonstrates on half of her how to go—when he does the throat cut I can see her wild eye and I want to tell her, *It's just the wool.* He hands the shears over to me. "Some places they have you hanging on a strap," he says, "save using your back too much. But if you don't use it it'll never get strong, so you'll just have to get used to that ache." And I do ache when the sheep starts struggling and whipping about and I have to hold her steady; I think I'm going to die from the ache afterwards. Because it is important, because if she is not still I will cut her skin, and she is eyeballing me like I'm going to slit her throat, and I want her to end this thinking, *Wasn't so bad.* I manage with a bit of help from Otto, who inspects my work afterwards.

"You've got to go deeper, girl—you're not close enough to the skin, leaving all that good stuff behind, stuff that binds it together. You need to peel her like an orange—pith and everythin'." And so on my second go the sheep gets cut, and it's horrible. When I see the blood I let her go, I can't believe I've held her down and hurt her and that she couldn't tell me. It is awful, it is awful, I never want to try it again, I can't, and Otto looks surprised when I cry but then he laughs good-naturedly. "Jesus Christ, girl, you might look like a man but you're sure not one, ay?" I haven't hated him before, but I do when he passes me the shears again and says, "C'mon, this is what you're here for," as if that were true, and he makes me catch the same one and I have to finish the job on that scared and bleeding sheep. "Here," he says, coming up behind and putting his arms around me to hold the sheep, "feel her wrapped around you," and I make the sheep fit in the hollow between my breasts and my hips, somehow, and she feels safe there, locked in. "Now," he says, holding up his hand, "breathe."

Twice more I make them bleed and then I get the angle, I get the understanding of it, and it *is* like taking the skin off an orange, or more accurately like peeling a mandarin, when the skin is thick and the pith attached and there is something satisfying about it, and when I do it right the sheep doesn't struggle or cry, it just lies there and lets me get on.

I spray the hose in my face to wash off the flies and they come back quickly to suck up the beads of water on my skin. I lean on the fence for a while, looking away from Otto's, watching the mirage, and I let myself believe it is the sea, and that the desert ends in a gentle slope down to the water's edge, which hides my house, with my people who are living in it. A rabbit shifts on the mirage and it's gone. A whistler circles above it.

I'm sweeping up, which is important with all the blue bottles. The amount of shit and maggots I've taken off the ewes is disgusting, and sweeping the great hunks of black wormy wool out the door is satisfying. Afterwards, I give myself another hose down. I put my thumb over the nozzle to try and get a stronger spray, and run the water over the dark stain under the meat hook. The pressure is not great and it doesn't have much of an effect. Water starts to run over the boards and into the corner of the shed, where the feed is kept in a large plastic barrel. I'm checking that there's nothing behind the barrel that shouldn't get wet and I find an earring. It's a small gold heart with a teardrop of opal hanging from it. It sits in my palm like a dead beetle. I put it back where I found it and cycle back to the house to make Otto his lunch. My hair dries before I'm back, and in the bathroom mirror I see the sun has worked me over, left me pink and brown, picked out the new bulges of muscle on my arms.

Later, back at the woolshed I roll up the fleeces, and I find some string to bind them all up neatly. When Otto comes out with the truck and I show him, he laughs.

"Pretty impressive, pet," he says, "but no one wants shit an' maggots in their carpets. Maybe on the next shear there'll be something better."

We load it up anyway and when we've driven back to the house, I help throw it all into the paddock. "All good fertiliser," he says, but I'm not sure I believe him. Kelly sits on her behind and when we've finished chucking them in, she goes to investigate, comes back with fleece sticking to her muzzle and a hacking cough from eating hair.

I think about the earring that night when Otto comes to me and bends me over the bed. I think about how he took my little penknife, which really couldn't do much damage to anyone, and how he never mentioned it to me.

While we are lying there in the aftermath and he is collecting himself, he tests one of my biceps, pinches it between his fingers.

"Getting some guns on you, girl. I like a useful body. Just don't go getting too manly." He laughs as if he has told a joke.

I can hear his guts churning in him because he had a late supper. I ask, "How long ago did Carole leave?"

He looks at me and there's something nettley in his eyes. "How come you want to know about that?"

I skate a hand over his windy chest and roll over, try to look cute, which is not easy for me. "I just wondered how long you had to cope all on your own out here. Must've been lonely?" And he softens, and closes his eyes, lets his head fall back, and relaxes after his exertions.

"She left probably a year before you came."

I want to ask more questions but I can't figure how to get away with it. I want to know what she looked like, how tall; the kind of woman to wear earrings on a sheep farm—what kind of woman is that?

"You don't need to worry about Carole," he says and wheezes out of his nostrils loudly, because there is detritus up there. "She was a slut. Not like you. You're a little girl in a slut's skin. She was the other way."

There's a small stereo in the telly room, and the CDs are mainly things like Slim Dusty and *Tales from the Mallee*, which I don't think much of, but among them are INXS and Cole Porter, and I know both those names. I put Cole Porter on and Otto comes in the house. "Course Carole always liked a dance," he says. I think that will mean I have to turn the music off, but he does a neat little four-step and takes my hand in his fingertips, turns me twice and then finishes with a little flourish, leaning me back like he's a gentleman. Kelly is barking at the door in fury, and out the fly-screen I catch her eye as he dips me. *I win this round, mother superior.*

I think of when I first arrived in Port Hedland with the pizza parlour bed-and-breakfast you could pay ten dollars to work out of, how the owner called us jobless sluts, giving her restaurant a bad name. But she still let us in for ten dollars, so long as we didn't use the towels, which you wouldn't anyway because they stank of smoke and sometimes they had a little trail of something wiped on them.

I feel hopeful here; even in those moments I'm searching the sky for an airplane, I think, can't complain, because it's been worse, much worse and the two of us laugh that night and drink a beer and Kelly sits outside in the dust, biting at her fleas. There is one last Holiday left in a packet I find stuffed into the pocket of my jeans, along with a book of matches. I hide it and think about it often, and wait for the moment when I need it most. It makes me feel better, just knowing it's there.

17

The fence around Don's lawn was decorated with more dead moles, some flapping in the wind, a few still moist enough to draw flies.

"Well," he said, "a visit from the hermit crab. You look better. Had a kip? Was going to drop by you later today in fact—bloody stupid woman at the fishmonger's keeps giving me fish. I hate the stuff—sort of rubbish your lot eat. She's gone sweet on me, silly cow, can't stop giving me her stinking flounder." He smiled at me. "Heard you made it down the pub the other week with your new fancy man."

"Samson came to see me the other night," I said, and Don's face sagged a little.

"Did he do anything?"

"No. Not really."

"Come in. Come in and I'll make you a coffee."

Don's kitchen was pine and chrome in a way that reminded me of hospitals. He turned on his electric kettle and made me watch as a light strip on its side turned from blue to purple to bright red.

"Ever see one of those before?" he asked.

"No, never," I said.

"Got that for nothing—came with the kitchen," he said and put a sachet of instant coffee in each mug. He added water and stirred. It was the kind of instant coffee that already had milk in it—it had a grey-looking head on it. "Seen that before?" he asked.

"No," I said. "It's great, isn't it?"

"Aye," said Don, looking proudly at his mug. "Aye, it is. They call it instantchino."

We sipped the coffee and I nodded appreciatively. "It's good," I said. It was not good. But Don looked pleased, and offered me one of his sweeteners from a tin that dropped them when you pressed a button. I took two to be polite and he nodded again.

"Margaret would have a conniption fit."

I smiled. The room was thick with the smell of our instantchinos.

Don sighed and said, "I'll bet you didn't know that Margaret was only forty-three when she died." His face had a look to it like he'd won a treasure hunt.

"I don't know anything about her," I said, though I had always thought of her as being Don's age, I realised—a timely death, sad, but not unexpected. Don lifted himself up out of his chair and went over to a drawer in the kitchen. Out of it he pulled a colour photograph: Don, looking much the same as he did now, the oilskin coat the same, the boots. A different shade of shirt on underneath the oilskin and a thicker quality to the white hair at the side of his head, but that was all. The woman next to him could have been his daughter, her blond hair in a ponytail, a long beaked nose and her mouth open, laughing. Her hand rested on the head of a small dark child, who held a fistful of her turquoise bomber jacket in his paw. The boy wore dungarees and had his hair parted to the side; he was maybe four years old, but I recognised the look, the deep frown and open mouth of Samson.

"Jesus," I said. "When was this taken?"

Don propped the photo up against the jug in the centre of the table. "About fifteen years ago." He drained the last of his coffee and leant back in his chair and clasped his hands behind his head.

"See," he said, "I always thought I'd go long before Margaret. Otherwise I wouldn't have said yes when she said she wanted the baby." Don's eyes were closed, like he was picturing the event. I looked at my coffee and wondered if I'd be able to finish it. The silence lengthened.

"I haven't been a good father to him," Don said softly. "Didn't know what to do in the first place. And that's all fine if you've got a loving mother—don't need the father so much then." He opened his eyes and looked at me. "Just like my old man." He swept one of his arms from behind his head like he was gesturing at something. "He was no damn good at it—he went to work and came home and we stayed out of his way." He let his hand find its way back behind his head. "I wasn't as bad as that—I wanted to be more than that to Samson, but I wasn't good at it. Couldn't do the baby talk, found it embarrassing. Margaret used to say to me, *He's not a short adult, he's a child.* But I never saw the difference. And then when he got older, there was trouble with his attention span or something. Teachers were no good. I was no good. But his mother—she was good." He dropped his hands down and laid them on the table, carefully. They were old hands, older than the rest of him. One of his index fingers had a scar all the way down it as if it had been split open, and the nails were yellow, thick and horny. The tips of his fingers pointed in strange directions.

"When she died Samson was sixteen. Where I'm from, that meant you were a man. I didn't know what to do with him—I don't know if he knew what to do with me either. We didn't know what to say to each other without her." Don bit his bottom lip and held it there. I listened to the sound of us breathing. "When he started with the fires, I thought he was punishing me, but I thought I'd done nothing wrong, so what was there to punish? I never brutalised him. Not once. Never did to him the things my father would've."

My mouth was dry, but I couldn't wet it with the instantchino which was lukewarm now and sickly.

"What did he set fire to?"

"Cars at first. Then a barn. Then he had a go at the cottage while I was in it, but I came down in the night and found him sitting over the table with his head in his hands. He'd made a little bonfire in the corner of the room, and I say, *What are you up to?* And he says he wants the place burnt. And so I called the police after that. On my own boy, on our boy."

Don looked far away.

"What did the police do?" I thought of the sergeant, gentle-eyed and useless.

"They said did I want to press charges, and even the fella whose barn Sam set alight—he hadn't pressed charges once I paid him back for it—even he said, the boy's just troubled after his mother. But I pressed charges, and the boy went to borstal."

I picked up my mug and drank the bad coffee just to have another movement, another noise in the room.

"I had it in my head the place'd do him some good, some rules, some toughening—Margaret was never big on those things. She thought we should nurture his dream to be a guitar player." Don laughed. "He was dreadful at that, purely dreadful. *He's my son,* I said; *he'll be a farmer.*"

Outside the sun came out from behind a cloud, so that it was like someone had opened a curtain in the room. I could see Midge through the window, resting her head on her paws, looking out towards my sheep. "And after he'd gone, when it was just me alone in the house without him to worry about, I began to see what he meant."

"What did he mean?"

"He meant to burn down the house, and I saw why."

I nodded, but all I could think of was the water in the tap over the sink, and how I'd like to pour away the coffee and take down large gulps.

150

"Memories?" I said.

Don looked up like he'd forgotten I was there. He smiled. "Woke up in the night with Midge howling outside, looked out the window and there she was, Margaret, in her dressing gown, the only clothes I took for her to the hospice. She had her back to the house, walking towards the woods, but I could see it was her."

I got up and poured away my coffee, rinsed my mug and filled it with water. I drank and listened as the water collected in my belly.

"I went down and outside, and I ran out with Midge going berserk alongside me, and I chased to the spot I'd seen her, saw something go into the woods and I just stood there calling for her. But she never came back. I thought about burning the place down then. Couldn't sleep for the fear she'd come back. Or wouldn't come back."

Don exhaled, rested his old head in his hand. "When Samson came out the borstal he didn't come and see me. I ran into him in town a few times, took him for a drink, said sorry. But there's things no amount of saying sorry'll fix. He's a gentle soul, really." He looked up at me. "He'd not do that to your sheep, if that's what you're thinking. I'm sorry he gave you a scare, but if your sheep are being slaughtered, it's an animal, it's not my son, I promise you that."

I gripped onto my mug and nodded. "I know it's not him," I said. Don's eyes were watery. "I've heard he sometimes camps in the woods, and I wanted to ask him if he's seen anything."

Don smiled. "He will have seen lots of things, though you have to pick your way between choosing what ones are real. I haven't got the hang of that, and I don't think I've got the time left in me to sort the real from the daydreams."

"He wants to see you—he was asking after you. That's why he came to the cottage—he didn't know you'd moved."

151

"He does know," Don said with a little shake of his head, "he just forgets things. Must be off his pills."

I thought about the look on Samson's face as he turned and walked into the dark.

"Yep, afraid I turned my son loopy," Don said and clasped his old hands around his mug.

I stood up to leave, felt my fists clenching at my sides. Without warning one of my hands rested itself on Don's shoulder, and I said, "I don't think it's your fault," and we stayed like that for an awkward moment. Don wiped an old wrist under his nose.

"Come and I'll give you this flounder this bloody woman gave me," he said, and got up to go to the fridge. "Me, I'll be having a Lean Cuisine."

18

The Aboriginal girl gets herself killed. Karen is smoking a Holiday and her hand is shaking. "I fucking told you, didn't I?" she says and she pours out a sloppy measure of Bi-Lo vodka into her mug of tea. There are rings of soot around her eyes. She gets this way sometimes. "Didn't I fucking tell you they do it for anything?"

I take the bottle from her and pour some into my can of Coke.

"Just makes it dangerous for the rest of us—giving these arseholes the idea in the first place, I mean fuck. No respect, no thought about the future. They don't try to educate themselves, they don't care where they're livin'." She sucks hard on her Holiday. "Fuck, they don't even care if they wake up in the morning. Well, that's where it gets you"—she slaps her thigh, hard—"throttled and fucked and stuffed in the back of a car." She drains her tea and starts to unscrew the bottle again, but midway through her face loses its hardness and crumples, her mouth bowing out at the sides like a child. "Christ," she says, though no tears come; she catches her breath and holds her palm to her chest. "She's just a kid." A high-pitched sound escapes from somewhere deep in her throat and I take the bottle out of her hand, put my hand in its place and sit there until she can breathe again. She pulls it together with a long sniff and looks in silence at the space over my shoulder. "We're not like that," she says. "We've got options—we're smart. Right? RIGHT?" She shouts a little and I nod. She swallows. "We're not dependent on this. It's a life choice." I nod after every statement. She looks at me. "You get the chance and you go," she says. "Opportunity is waiting around every corner." So is death, I think, but I don't say it out loud.

I'm sitting in the Macquarie Lanes Diner as usual with one of my regulars, Otto. Otto is good because he's twice a month, a fair price, and there's never any fighting about it. He doesn't want to do those games the others like to do, he doesn't want to pretend he's getting something from me for free, and he doesn't offer to pay me double if he can hit me in the face while we're doing it. Sometimes, with no reason to it, the pre-stuffed envelope of ten-dollar notes is more than the price we agreed at the start six months ago. All he wants to do is talk for a couple of hours and then he wants one bit of sex, either a blowie or a normal. He pays me enough that I don't have to work the rest of the night, which is the real prize. Afterwards he buys me my tea in the diner and he eats too, not like the bleeding hearts who take me for food and order for me, way too much, and then sit there watching, making me feel like a disgusting pig while they sip at a beer, or a black coffee if they're the Christian type. I've got thin at the Hedland. It makes me feel neater, easier to pack away.

Otto's wife left him, he tells me, "like a pig prancing out of a pen."

He owns a sheep station close to Marble Bar, a few hours' drive from the Hedland. "It's a beaut spot," he says. "Green in the winter, good watering hole to swim in in the summer. Course, I try and be self-sufficient, as much as possible—a bit of grow-your-own—heck, there's enough space!" he says, and chuckles. I imagine it, the fat woolly sheep, the rows of carrots and strawberries sprouting out of the ground. The fruit trees. I think up a tyre-swing and hang it over the watering hole, imagine ducks landing there on their way over. The sound of frogs at night. "Just me an' the

154

missus out there," he laughs. "That's Kelly, me dog—she's like a sister to me." He takes out his wallet and shows me a picture of her, she's got beady eyes and sharp ears. "Not one of those sheep'd put a foot wrong while she's in charge, wouldn't no bastard fox take a go either. She'd rip the skin off 'em." Otto dips four chips in sauce and puts them all in at once. He enjoys the food at the diner because, he says, "Can't cook for buggery. Carole used to do all that, eggs, snags, chops—the whole piece. I'm more of a corned beef and beans cook. Fuckin' awful."

With Otto I always order the calamari with a salad. The salad is the type with grated carrot and beetroot, not the type you see in the picture on the menu with the prickly-looking green leaves and tiny tomatoes and cucumber, but it's all the same to me. Important, I know, to have a salad, it's what me and Karen have when we eat together on off-nights.

When other people order for me, like they either worry I'd be too shy or too greedy, they always get me the beefburger and chips. They don't think for a moment I might be a vegetarian, as if I'd be allowed to have those choices.

Tonight I have the fruit for afters, which is tinned, but it's still good for you. Good for your skin, I think to myself every time, as if the welts on my back might heal over if I only have enough vitamins.

Because of the issue of space in Otto's cab, and also because of the dark, he's never seen my back. Because he never tells me *Turn over*, it has never been an issue. Sometimes we feel like friends. Today was blowie day, but not one of those punch-down-the-throat ones people are so fond of. I appreciate this because it can make the next one a real piece of hard work, it can bring tears to your eyes just swallowing.

I finish my calamari and my plate is beet-stained and greasy, and I have a beer, because you want something to cut through the feeling in your throat, even if it's from a nice bloke like Otto. And then he fixes me with a beady eye, and he says, "Listen, pet, I've got a proposition."

I leave a message for Karen, because she's out when I run home to pack a bag. It'll probably just be a week, *Just a short break to see if I like the idea*. I leave Karen money for the rent for the next month just in case—that's Otto's idea and he gives the money to me in twenties. He insists on leaving more than the rent costs, "So she knows I'm for real," he says. I tell Karen in the note that I'll call the phone in the hall if I stay longer, and she can come and visit. I know she'll understand, it's what she's after herself—to be out.

19

When I stopped at the top field on the way back home, I was missing a sheep. I counted and recounted five times and came up short. I searched the perimeter fence and the drainage ditch and there was no sign. The fence was solid. It was like something had swooped down and lifted her off.

I cut at a section of bramble that had got tangled around the nose and upper jaw of an old ewe. She was from my first lot, mature when she came to me. I was surprised the last time she managed a pregnancy, but this year she remained uninflated.

I forced open her jaw and cut the bramble out. It had made deep welts around her snout and done who knows what inside her mouth. She rolled her eyes away from me and towards the rest of the flock, struggling between my thighs until I let her go. The mud had made it in through the holes in my boots, and the old ewe bustled off without a glance behind her, without even the slightest air of being grateful that I had taken the thorns out of her face.

"Screw you then!" I shouted at her, and she stopped walking but didn't turn back to look at me. I kicked the gate closed behind me and took a shortcut up through the row of blackthorn and came out at the foot of the downs with the wind at my back. It pushed behind me and I ran in my clunking boots up the slope with flint and chalk loosening under my steps and with rabbits darting in and out of the brambles to my side. At the top I sweated and caught my breath while I inspected the southern sweep of the fields. Nothing moved other than the treetops. I turned to look out at the mainland and sat down to light a cigarette. I watched the car ferry crossing the water, a small white shoebox, and beyond that, the mainland waiting like a crocodile with all those people on its back.

To the west, the concrete wall of the island's prison came out of the woods, and in a few places the Military Road was visible. Soon, once spring came in, the road would be invisible, the prison gone.

A movement caught my eye past the blackthorn at the foot of the slope. I stood up hoping to see my lost sheep, but it was Lloyd, digging. I watched for a while, his great sweeping movements, letting the spade take its own weight as it cut through the heavy wet ground. Dog lay next to him, watching, his head on his paws. Lloyd had his back to me. He was singing something, I caught a note on the wind. He looked right with a shovel, alone in the pit of the hill.

A light spit came on, or it could have been sea spray, lifted over the cliffs by the wind. Dog described a circle around the spot Lloyd worked on, smelling and nosing the things that were unearthed. I walked down towards them, not sure what I would say when I reached them. Lloyd squatted and pulled something from the hole which caught Dog's attention. He trotted over and smelled it for Lloyd, who touched Dog's head in acknowledgement. Dog returned to his business, and Lloyd weighed whatever it was in his hands like a fillet of beef and then threw it to the side. His shoulders tensed. I stopped and followed his gaze up into the white sky, where a merlin hovered. They eyeballed each other. Lloyd started to sing at the bird, but all that reached me on the breeze was a murmur. He dropped his shovel and flung both arms out, the wind blew his hair so that it stood straight up at the back, wild and grey. He did a little dance and the bird dropped down lower to watch. He sang louder, he howled, "I wish that every kiss was never-ending!" and a bellow of wind came up behind me and blew my hair over my face. A second later it hit Lloyd and he wobbled in his dance, patted his hair back onto his head and turned towards me. *The human eye senses movement before all else.* Lloyd raised his hand at me and I raised mine at him. He looked up for his bird, which had let itself be blown away by the wind. He scanned the empty sky a moment longer, then sat down with his back to me, next to the hole he'd dug. Dog stood and barked once, and I made my way down to them.

"Digging a hole?" I asked.

"Is it okay?" said Lloyd.

"What are you burying?"

"I'm just digging." He kept staring up at the spot where the bird had been. There was silence, and I sat down next to him.

Dog tried to lick my face but I pushed him away.

"Seeds," he said.

"What are?"

"I was going to plant some apple seeds." There was silence again.

"Okay."

To prove himself, Lloyd took an apple out of his pocket and turned it in his hand in front of me. "Ha!" he said, then flung the apple as far as he could into the blackthorns. There was more silence and then he said, "When I was a kid I was into reincarnation."

I caught the smell of whisky. "Seems like a comforting thing to think," I said, for something to say.

"I'm not sure I believe in it now. But I like to pretend I do."

He was really going to get in the way once the lambs started coming.

"Do you believe in an after-life?" he asked with another gust of his whisky breath.

"No I don't."

"Then what are you so frightened of?"

I stared at him. His eyes were glassy.

"So the seeds?" I said. "Tell me about the seeds."

He leant back and breathed in harshly through his nose and closed his eyes. "In remembrance."

"Of what?"

"The Jews do it. The tree of life; they call it something, the holiday. The Queen does it too—she plants a tree."

Dog whined. I fidgeted. Lloyd closed his eyes. The wind dropped and the whole place slowed down.

"I'm sorry," he said. "I'm not making the best sense." He inhaled deeply. "It was nothing special," he said, his eyes popping open. "He was alive in the morning and then by the afternoon he was suddenly dead."

"Who?"

He pointed to the empty space where the bird had hovered.

I twisted a blade of grass until it produced juice. Lloyd took from his carrier bag a quarter-empty bottle of whisky. He took a swallow that was longer than would have been comfortable in the throat. He wiped the top off with the underside of his wrist and offered it to me. I nearly said no, but I didn't.

"Look—I've got the last of his ashes in an envelope." He took from his breast pocket a small packet that looked badly weathered. "But they got wet. He's more mud now than ash."

160

Lloyd looked inside the packet and then refolded it and sighed. He sat himself up straight, and spoke with a new authority. "The idea was I'd go to the furthest points of Britain. This was my last stop. I do a little ceremony at each place—the first three were okay. I went to Suffolk and I had a little toy wooden sailboat, and I set it on fire with a little bit of him on board. It was dark and the sea was flat and nobody was there, and it went so well." He smiled and closed his eyes again. "I watched until he was out of sight and I thought, when this is done, I will feel better."

A large moth wobbled between us. I watched it settle for a moment in Lloyd's beard and then take off again in the direction of the sun.

"John O'Groats!" Lloyd barked, opened his eyes and gave me a look like I was arguing with him. I picked up the bottle from where it sat next to him and drank a little more. It was smokier than I liked.

"At John O'Groats I made a circle out of stones and sprinkled him all over them. Like decorating a cake. That was nice. I sat down next to him and drank champagne. And then I threw him off a cliff edge in Cornwall. It was all good. But here— I can't get this last one right." He looked at me, crestfallen. "I'm bored of it, sick of it." He looked at the envelope in his hands. "I could just pass by a bin outside a chip shop and drop him in."

"Who was he?" My throat was burning.

"He was mine," Lloyd said, and smiled widely. "He was mine and he was hit by a truck on his way to work. BAM!" he shouted, and giggled and then was quiet.

"Your son?"

"No—not my son."

20

Working at the Hedland is different from Darwin. In Darwin someone told me it was safer at the Hedland where there were fewer tourists who came and went, and that the sex was more average because they were the people who lived and worked there. At the Hedland, they weren't off their tits on excitement because they were on holiday. It made sense, and I did some reading up on the place, which is a mining town, and so I expected it to look like a Western film, but when I got off the Greyhound it looked just like a shitty little town. And as it goes, the sex is just the same for bored men as it is for over-excited men. I guess they've had the chance to really think about the things they'd like to do to a person. But not all of them are like that. Some are kind, but even kind people use other people for sex. You come to see that.

I share a room and a bed above a rotisserie chicken shop with Karen. She's been in Port Hedland two years by the time I get there, but she doesn't tell me why, and I don't tell her why I'm there either. We just rub along together, and she makes me laugh. She's the beautiful type, straight out of a magazine, with long hair and a small waist, and I try not to think too hard about how she, looking like she does, could have come to be in the same place as me.

We try and make the place look decent, even if it smells bad from all the cooked chickens, and Karen refers to a thing she calls "ombionce" which is brought about by scented candles and a red and orange rag rug over the only window. She also talks about "fung shuay" and throws a fit when I move things around while she's out, so that the foot of the bed faces the door. "That's how you get carried out when you die!" she wails, yanking the bed across the room to where it had been before, so it gets in the way every time you walk by it, and you smash your shin on it.

"So what?" I say. "You'd rather go headfirst out the window?" She doesn't laugh.

We try not to bring work back to the room, both of us prefer to work in a bloke's truck or their place, but sometimes if it's cold out you get more done if you can take them somewhere yourself, so we figure out a rota so that she gets the odd hours, I get the even. She works harder than I do, she says she has a hunger to get out of the Hedland. One afternoon we're sipping Cokes and ice outside the Four Square on the main street, and Karen points to an Aboriginal girl down an alleyway, leant up against the fence, her eyes closed with the sun in them.

"See her," says Karen, "that's what we got below us. That's the level down. Those girls haven't got the drive to get to a better place than this." I look at the girl she's nodding at, a girl about my age, or maybe younger, wearing a soft blue T-shirt and a skirt that doesn't look comfortable to wear. "That one there, I've seen her go for a can of beer." She turns to me and says in a softer voice, one that I'm not used to hearing come out of her, "Don't ever think that we're stuck here like her, we're not, we got a way out if we want it."

Karen gets picked up pretty soon after that, and I stay there looking at the girl who screws for beer money and I wonder what the difference is. She sees me looking and faces me with her two feet planted apart, and stares back in a way that lets me know there is something different there, but not something I know anything about. I move along, because she scares me.

*   *   *

164

For a couple of months the Hedland feels safe. I can walk around and I don't feel eyes on me. I sleep, I don't wake up and have that feeling someone's crouched in the corner, that they've slunk in the window and they've been waiting for me to see them. But on my way to work one night I'm aware of the sound of footsteps close behind me. When I hurry, they speed up. The main thing is not to look, and I push into an all-night café. No one follows me in and I sit on a Coke for an hour and then the waitress starts staring at me and it could be because I've only bought a Coke and I've stayed too long. She starts walking towards me with a sour look on her face, and an older bloke with a thick middle comes up and sits with me.

"She's all right, Marg," he says, "she's with me." He smiles at me in a way I haven't seen in a long time, and the waitress rolls her eyes and goes back behind the counter. "Beer for your thoughts?" he asks and gets the waitress to bring two. He's lonely, and you can tell that he's not just worried about getting his leg over, he's worried about talking to someone.

"Was reading here," he says, showing me his newspaper, "about how they found a six-foot carpet snake under this old lady's bed—she'd been dropping food down for her cat when her nurse brought it in. Snake ate the cat and then ate the leftovers too probably!" He laughs and I laugh too. The waitress looks over.

"I always wanted a pet at home," I say but I shut up about that because the word makes me feel hot and sad. "You live far from here?" I ask the man, wondering if he will try to pick me up later.

"Yeah. Fair way," he says. "Come into town now and again for some decent food and stave off the boredom. Was in town tonight to see a film as it goes."

"What are you going to see?"

"Missed it now. They were doing *Lady and the Tramp*—loved that film."

I smile. He's a soft old git. "Sorry if I made you miss it."

"Nah," he blushes a little, "don't be sorry. It's a treat to talk to someone."

When we finish our drinks he doesn't ask for anything, or try to make me stay with another drink. He just tells me to keep safe. "I'm in here every few weeks," he says, "if you ever want a talk and a beer—a night off." He shakes me by the hand. "It's been a pleasure talking with you. Name's Otto, hope we'll meet again." He slips me $20 and leaves $10 on the counter for our drinks, then leaves the café without even a squeeze at my boobs. When he walks he goes from side to side as well as forward.

"The way I see it," says Karen, lighting the second half of her last cigarette, "is that you just go straight down. You just dig to China."

I frown. "China's to the side."

"It's a figure of speech." Karen frowns back and inhales the stale cigarette, passes it to me and I know we are friends. "England, then. If you want to be specific about it. The main point is, we're not supposed to be here, us whiteys. The place is trying to spit us out all the time." I pass the cigarette back, careful not to take more than is polite. Karen puts it in her mouth and leans forward at me, pointing to her lip, almost burning me with the tip of the cigarette.

"See this?" There's a small white scar there. "I'm twenty-three, I had a cancer burnt off there last year." She sits back, holds the smoke in her lungs and lets it out in waves. She folds her arms in front of her. "Who knows what else is going on with my face right now." She feels her cheeks like she's looking for bits that will

166

fall off. "Did you know our mum never gave us anything to cover over our faces? And that was the era of Slip Slop Slap—we did a whole fuckin' school assembly on it." She stands up and does a little performance. "'Slip! Slop! Slap!'" she sings. "'Slip on a shirt, slop on sunscreen and slap on a hat.'" She does a turn and some jazz hands, then stands on one hip with her arms folded. "I was the bloody bird—even then, *even then* she couldn't be bothered to zinc us up."

"You want a cup of tea?" I ask, getting up off the floor.

"This is our problem, right, I've worked it out," she says, not listening. I put the kettle on the stove anyway. "We shouldn't be here, we shouldn't have come to Australia to start with. Look at us—crusted with skin cancers. The sea wants to kill us, the bush wants to kill us. You know there's a shell in the north—you pick it up on a beach, thinking you've found something pretty to hang round your neck, the fucker shoots out a poison arrow that'll disintegrate your kidneys? It's fucked, and we shouldn't be here." Karen points the dying end of her cigarette at me again. "You—you are not supposed to go into the sea—it's like a nest of snakes in there." She lets her head loll back and says quietly, "Fuck it, even the dry bits are a nest of snakes."

"You want mint tea or regular?"

Karen sighs, flings up her arms without looking at me. "I want flaming English Breakfast Tea! And a scone!"

"Well, we're out of milk."

"For god's SAKE!"

I like it when she gets like this, it's better than watching TV. She leans up to accept her black tea. "I wish I had some mull," she says dejectedly. I pour hot water over a regular tea bag. She blows into her mug and then takes a sip, grimaces, sighs again and sets the mug on the floor, where it spills over a little. She looks at the burnt-out end of her cigarette and puts it back

167

in the empty packet. I try not to worry about the thing still being alight.

"In England," she goes on, "they take teatime seriously. Know what a Devon cream tea is?"

I shake my head and let the steam from my drink work over my face. It's hard to take my eyes off the cigarette packet, to not think about what is going on inside, what tiny spark might be left.

She leans forward and cups her hand like she's holding something. "They take a scone, some jam and some cream, and they make little scone sandwiches out of them."

"Doesn't sound all that exciting to me."

"But that's the point!" she says, showing me the palms of her hands. "They make eating a boring little cake a real event. With parasol umbrellas and silverware. You can do a Devon cream tea on a boat, going down the river, or you do it on a lawn."

"I'd rather be fishing if I'm on a boat," I say just to rile her, and also to distract from the fact that I've stood up to take her cigarette packet. I empty out the burnt stub and run it under the tap in the sink.

She flaps her hands. "But that's my point, exactly." She gets wet-eyed and earnest. "You take the time to do things, gentle things, you make the *act* of having teatime a beautiful thing. Here"—she smiles, picks up a box of crackers from the side table that we've reserved for dinner—"here, we've got fuckin' *Chicken Crimpies.*"

Usually the Hedland is baking dry, but out of nowhere one evening there's a cyclone, which lasts a week. It's pelting rain outside, and so if a bloke doesn't want to do it in his car, me and Karen have to use the room or else hire one out at the pizza parlour, which is a waste of money. We have only two sets of sheets, so it's a question of being careful, putting down a towel and *leaving the place as you'd expect to find it.* Karen takes down her poster of a unicorn, because she says men don't find that sort of thing sexy. Above the bed is a depressing picture made out of wood shavings. It's a cattle station, or it's supposed to be. Just looks like wood shavings to me, but because it was there when we moved in and because it is in a frame, and because behind the picture there's a gash in the wall where someone's thrown something heavy, we keep it there. I have a sneaking suspicion that Karen likes it and thinks it adds to the *ombionce.*

It's still stinking hot, even with the rain pouring down, and we're both busier than we would normally be—I suppose people get bored when they can't go out, I suppose they get thinking about other things, and then they want to have sex with a girl. We get in a muddle because, firstly, once you get into the room and the two of you are soaked, it's rude not to give them a towel, and by the time you've both dried off enough to get down to it, part of the time is ticking away, but you can't tell them that, they won't have it. As far as they are concerned the hour they buy is an hour of sex, and if it happens to be raining hard enough to soak you to your undies, then that's your bad luck. A couple of times I walk in on Karen and she walks in on me, so we take to hanging a bead necklace on the door handle if we are in and working. Sometimes it means waiting around in the hall and making conversation with the bloke, while you can both hear the squeakings and the gruntings that are going on inside the room. Sometimes it puts a bloke off, but all in all it is better than having someone walk in on you, because now and then he'll turn nasty if that happens. Like his mum's walked in on him or something.

I'm there with a man who calls himself Simon, though I can see he's written his name on the inside of his work boots when he takes them off and in his boots he calls himself the Rock—written in curly letters, like he thinks he's a super-hero or something. I reckon from the way he goes on about how great he is, he might have given himself that nickname. Me and the Rock get up on the bed and it's all pretty usual with me on top.

"Keep yer bra on." The Rock has a thing for tits in a bra. He grabs on them while he's bucking away underneath me, and he keeps his eyes firmly on the cleavage he's made himself by squashing them together. His tongue pokes out of his mouth, like a kid colouring in. His concentration gives me the chance to have a quick look at my watch—I graze it past my face and then pretend to be all about the sex and grab my hair and put my finger in my mouth. It's getting late, Karen'll be back in ten, and this guy's not going to get very far with my boobs. If I concentrate I think I can hear her outside, and it's embarrassing when that happens.

Just then he says, "Tell me you want me to come on your tits." And just the idea of me saying this makes him do an extra big thrust, which punches me in the gut so that I want to smack him right in the face. The thrust is so large that it bangs the bedhead against the wall, and the crappy wood-chip picture bumps a little, and all of a sudden out from the crack in the wall behind it come dozens of baby huntsmen. It takes me a second to react and in that second the Rock does another super-thrust, and when it bangs the wall a spider falls right into his face and he screams, and I scream and jump off him, and he leaps for the floor, scrubbing his face with his hands, dancing about and shouting, "Fuck fuck fuck!" like he's burning. There's a pounding on the door, and it smashes open and it's Karen wide-eyed after hearing the commotion, she's taken her shoe off and is holding it ready to beat the eyes out of whoever is murdering me, and she sees the

170

spiders and yells, and I see a man behind her pelting his way down the stairs and out of the building. The Rock is standing at our sink washing his face over and over and the spiders are still spewing out and spreading all over the wall. Me and Karen yell and yell, and we start laughing, and the Rock turns around with tears in his eyes and spits, "Fucking whores!" like we bred the spiders especially, and then he shakes his trousers and gets into them, jumping about like he has them all over, when the only place they are, apart from the one that fell on his face, is all over the wall. "You can forget about the money, you fuckin' witch!" he spits and pegs out of the room with his boots in his hand and I shout after him, "Bye, the Rock!" and me and Karen fall on each other laughing, and screaming, because our room is covered in tiny spiders.

The dream is nothing special. It's just a dream of home. I can smell it. I can smell the old chip-fryer and Mum's secret smoke behind the house. The triplets are a background noise of wants and fighting, the closeness of a full house. I'm in the bathroom, I'm lying in the bath but I can still see through to the room I share with Iris, and Iris is in there pashing with some boy. The house is trying to be normal but I know there is someone standing behind me that I can't see. That is all it is, but I wake up with Karen sitting on my chest, gripping my arms to my sides with her thighs, and clapping in front of my face and saying my name.

"Shit and Christ," she says, "what is it?" She climbs off and puts on the ombiant lamp that lives on the floor and has a red bulb. She looks back for an answer and her face is puffy from sleep. She sighs when I don't answer and pulls up her pillow so she can lean back and she lights two Holidays, passes me one. My heart is still fast and there's sweat on my face.

"Sorry," I say, and she looks at me sideways as she blows smoke out. "It was just a dream."

"No shit," says Karen, and she holds the smoke between her lips and moves a leaf of hair from my face. "You okay?"

I nod and, as my heart starts to slow, it feels like the dream is the smoke I breathe out. But the feeling is still there, the smell of the fryer in my nose. I practise closing my eyes and every time I do I see Iris through the knot in the bathroom wall. I feel my shoulders against the white curve of the bath, and I open my eyes again to replace the image with the one on our wall—the unicorn with the dolphins leaping behind him. He looks silly in the head.

"You want to talk?" asks Karen.

"No. Thanks." Karen crushes out her Holiday and then takes mine from me. She puts that out on the saucer by the ombiance lamp, and then switches the lamp off. Light eases in from behind the towels hung on the window. She shifts further up the headboard so she's sitting up, and then she surprises me by pulling me onto her so that her arm is around my back and my head is on her chest. I'm wary of hurting her boobs with my head, but she feels relaxed under me. I try to be too.

"Think of your brain," she tells me. "Visualise it." I can hear her breathing deeply in the dark, and it's nice. "Can you see it?" she asks.

"Okay," I say. My brain is neon pink and bulging.

"See the cleft that runs down the middle? That separates your brain into two halves?"

"I do." I zoom in on the line in my head.

"Think of it," says Karen; "that line is the corridor of your brain."

My imagined brain doesn't know what to do, so it just pulsates.

"Either side of the corridor," she goes on, and she starts to stroke my hair with the hand that's scooped around my back, "are the rooms with the memories in." Her voice has dropped a bit, and coupled with her breathing, in and out like the feeling of lying in the bottom of a boat in a gentle swell, it's easier to see the brain corridor. It's lit with halogen bulbs, and the floor is shiny, like a hospital corridor. There's no one in it, and it stretches on until it disappears out of sight. Karen starts to stroke my hair behind my ear, again and again. "Go in through one of those doors," she says. I reach out and when I look down, I'm dressed in an old-fashioned nursing outfit. My shoes are rubber-soled. I turn the door handle and step inside, where I see the bathroom back home and the little knot of wood that I can push out to watch Iris, but it is plugged with loo roll. Outside it is daytime, but also black. I can smell the world around me melting, I can smell the oil in the deep-fat fryer from downstairs, I hear a tinkle of glass breaking.

"And now step out of that room, via the door you went in through," says Karen, and I turn around, and the hospital door is still there, hasn't closed up while I wasn't looking, and I step my rubber-soled foot through it and into the dim-lit corridor. "And now close the door behind you and lock it." I take a large ring of keys from my crisp white pocket, and it jangles as I lock the door.

"And now walk down the corridor," says Karen and her fingers have started to slide deeper into my hair, stroking slowly in time with her breath, and she has slid down a little lower so that I feel her breath in my hair and it feels like hot bread, "and choose a new door. Open it. And go in, go into a good place. And if it turns into a bad room, leave, and find a new door."

I stand at the door with my keys in my hand. I can see my reflection in the safety glass. There's one of those little paper hats with the red cross on my head. Through the window I can see

21

I fried flounder in butter and we had it with bread. The sheep was still missing; how long would it be before she showed up as clumps of blooded wool dotted over the hillside? Lloyd was drunk, and I tried to get there too. When we'd walked up the driveway together, Lloyd sprinkling ashes from his envelope as he went so that his fingertips were black, something shrieked and it echoed across the valley. The hair at the back of my neck stood on end. Lloyd noticed nothing, sang his song.

While I cooked, he beetled around making a fire. I pretended not to notice when he unbalanced and had to sit cross-legged in the hearth to build it. He folded up the envelope and pushed it into the centre of his unlit fire, and then set a match to it. It was damp and so it took a few tries, and I felt sad for him that it hadn't all happened in a more satisfying way. He sat on the sofa once the fire had lit, singing again. "'Wouldn't it be nice if we were older, then we wouldn't have to wait so long,'" but his song was slow like a hymn.

Lloyd's beard had ashes in it, and he only shrugged when I told him, and left them there. The fish was good and the bread mopped up the whisky inside me. We didn't speak, just the scrape of forks on plates, the gullet swallow of our drinks, and of our glasses being refilled. Outside the rustle of the wind in the trees and now and again a howl that could have been the wind whistling through the valley, from off the sea through the black-thorn, down into the field of sheep feeding in the dark, and opening its mouth wide to swallow the house. We drank more and kept drinking.

"God, I wish you'd get a haircut," he said.

I stood up and swiped at his face, but I only clipped his ear, and he grabbed me round the wrist.

"Fucking hell!" he shouted. "Just a trim!"

I went to bed.

I woke in the morning with a dry mouth. Downstairs, the fire was just a glow and I fed it with the logs Lloyd had leant against the hearth. Dog was coiled on the other side of him in a deep sleep. I felt a long pulse of nausea from my stomach to my throat and my head, and drank three glasses of water and lit a cigarette. I smoked staring out the window at where the light was starting, pale grey. A late bat whipped around in front of the house and then disappeared under the eaves. No mist today, but a crispness, frost on the ground.

At first I thought it was a cat, because it moved in that way, loped like a cat, but it was larger and even this far away from the woods I could see the hair on its back was thick and wiry, its shoulders dense and muscled.

"Lloyd," I said, but not loud enough. It entered the dark bank of the woods and was gone. I blinked and wondered if I had seen anything at all.

At the shed I filled up the water and feed troughs. The daylight had started to go already and Dog lay down and moaned because he hadn't eaten yet. It was warm in the shed, and rain on the tin roof mingled with the bustle of the ewes finding their comfort in the straw. It smelled good. Lloyd touched the nose of a ewe I thought would have triplets. She snorted his hand away, but he didn't flinch. These ones at least were safe for now. I shifted the feed barrel to get to a new box of gloves behind it, and on the floor was a dainty hoof. I stared at it a moment before I understood what it was.

"Lloyd," I said and he came and stood next to me. We both looked at the foot, the bone crunched through at the ankle, the cleft toenails curled. "I'm going to sleep in here tonight."

"Whisky" was all he said.

22

In Darwin, a man with deep pockmarks on his chin and a smell about him like he's been infused with some kind of pickling vinegar offers me forty-five bucks, but not just for a blowie.

"The real thing," he says. Forty-five dollars does not seem like all that much, when that first one had given me thirty just to use my face.

"Fifty-five dollars?" I ask and he smiles at me like he is my indulgent father.

"We'll see how you go. You'd better be pretty good for fifty-five."

I don't know what to do. With the blowies it is fairly straight-forward—I kneel, they unzip. But we stand opposite each other a little while, me shifting from foot to foot.

"Where'll we do it?" I ask, finding that I am blushing.

"Got a tarp stretched over the back of the ute," he says and turns towards the road. His ute is a rusted thing with Queensland plates and a crack in the windscreen that has been reinforced with packing tape. A bright blue tarp is tented in the back tray like a kid's clubhouse. I stand on the step and go to get in.

"Not here, girl!" he snaps. "If I'm paying through the nose I want to make noise." And he climbs into the cab. I pull myself up on the other side and get in too. As we drive out of town, I feel nervous.

"What's your name?" I ask.

"Not your business."

There's a pause.

"My name's Jake."

"I don't want to talk."

"I come from over west, near Brisket."

"Never heard of it—Jesus, do I have to pay you to shut up as well?"

I decide his name is Ken, short for Kenneth. He probably works on a prawn trawler. He is the sort of character who is grouchy but ultimately friendly.

The rest of the ride is silent, and we pull into a car park at the beach, and he draws up under some fir trees.

"Git in the back," says Ken.

As I climb in under the tarpaulin, Ken pushes his hands against my bum and squeezes. It seems a strangely affectionate thing to do after being such a ratbag in the cab. Underneath the tarp everything is light blue and glowing. Ken and his skin and me and my skin all look illuminated, and his teeth look very white against his green face. It's warm in there with the sun making it smell of hot plastic. I smile at Ken and he holds my ankles and turns me over, not that gently, so that I can't see his face.

"Take em off," he says and I feel down to unbutton my shorts. It's embarrassing, the idea of getting your bum out at some man you don't even know. But I manage it, and he tugs them down and all of a sudden he is hot and damp and all over me, pushing and squeezing parts of him into me and swearing all the time he does it.

"Up," he says and pulls on my hips, so that I am on all fours, and he grunts into me. "Make some fuckin' noise," he says, and so I bang on the floor of the ute with my fists. "Not that sort of noise, you retard," he shouts, before I understand what he means. It's a strange thing making the noises he's after. There is an eyelet in the tarp which shows how white it is outside and I watch that

179

and make the noises he wants, pleased that my back is turned to him so that I don't also have to make the faces as well.

Grunting away and saying encouraging things like "Yeah, like that," Ken strokes my midriff in a way that could almost be friendly. He reaches up and feels my boobs under my T-shirt, and then back down the sides of me to where he is working away. He is starting to gasp and between us there is a racket of moans and shouts while I look at the white circle of sky. He presses his thumbs into the dips of my haunches, and then screams and falls backwards off me.

"What the fuck've you got!" he shouts with the air that's left in his throat. I turn around to look at him. He looks so angry with his trousers round his ankles and his dick cuddling up to him that I nearly laugh, and he kicks at me with his tethered legs.

"What is it, girl? Fuck I didn't even wear a rubber."

"I don't know what you mean," I try to say, and he almost throws me out of the back tray into the white, with my shorts around my knees and his wetness all on me. He charges out of the truck a moment later, as I am pulling my clothes back on and I think he's going to hit me, he comes so close to my face.

"What the fuck is that on your back?"

"Just scars," I say.

"Scars? From what?" He looks suspicious but his fists have relaxed. I shrug.

"An accident."

"What kind of *accident*?"

I don't know how to answer so I stand there, scratching my arm for a bit.

"An accident at sea," I say finally, because the words feel good to say and that is where the worst things happen.

He presses the heels of his palms to his eyes. "Fuck," he whistles quietly, "thought it was some sort of AIDS." And he spits on the ground next to me. "You should tell people you got that. It's not fair to make people pay for damaged goods."

Kenneth turns without giving me any money and gets into his truck. He drives away without a glance in my direction and just as I realise I've left all my stuff in the cab, I see my bag sail out of the window to land in the road. I collect up my things and stuff them back in, check to see if maybe he's put my thongs in too, but he hasn't. I walk back into town barefoot with bits of melted bitumen sticking to my heels. I haven't thought about my back like that before, that other people will see it and ask what it is. It was my first go at having lie-down sex, how was I supposed to know which bits have to be unscarred, which bits you can get away with.

23

The crows roosted in the treetops. Their blackness against the darkening sky made me want to get the gun and scatter them. From the house, I took a gas lamp so we wouldn't have to keep the fluorescent on, the last of the bread, which was stale, and some butter and honey. I put the coffee pot on the stove to fill up the thermos. Out the window, the light faded in waves, the tree branches became longer, hanging on to their shadows. I found two of my thickest jumpers and wrapped a half-bottle of whisky in one before I put it into my bag. I pulled out the box of cartridges I kept at the back of the kitchen cupboard. I took one out and weighed it in my hand. Dad trying to teach me to shoot cans out the back when I was small. He'd given me a cushion to hold against my shoulder so the recoil didn't leave a mark and Mum wouldn't throw a drama. "Remember," he'd said close to my ear, the soft gust of beer on his breath, "the human eye senses movement before all else."

The triplets had run out into the garden then, like a pack of baboons and Dad and I had pretended to pick them off one by one until Iris had leant out the window and shouted at us, "Stop it, you fucking derelicts!"

I closed my fist around the cartridge.

It was too early to call, and too close to the last time. But if it was Iris who answered, she'd hang up straight off anyway. I held the phone in one hand, the cartridge in the other, squeezing. It rang a long time and I imagined Mum getting out of bed, wrapping herself in her dressing gown and rubbing the sleep from her eyes. Phone calls at unusual hours were always bad news; I should have waited, she'd be worried. The voice when it picked up was deep and unfamiliar, a man's. For a second I thought Dad was alive after all, it had all been a trick. He didn't answer with Mum's usual *Hello, 635?* He said, "Yep?"

I opened my mouth and almost responded.

The man sniffed. "You there?" he said. When I left, the triplets were small boys. Now I supposed they were not. The voice cleared its throat, there was the muffled sound of the earpiece being smothered by something, like he held it to his shirt front. Maybe it was early enough to be cool in the house, maybe he wore a jumper, or a sweatshirt with a hood.

"Mum?" I heard him call away from the speaker, not over-loudly, but like he was testing, seeing who was near him. "Iris?" There was no response that I could hear. His voice came back to me. "Listen, I'll get the money, okay? Message understood, loud and clear, I'll have it by the end of the week. Please don't call here, it's got nothing to do with me mum—she's not well. End of the week, I promise, man—"

"Who in hell are you—?" I heard Iris close in the background and the phone slammed down in its cradle fast and loud enough that the line crackled before it went dead. I looked at the receiver in my hand and lowered it gently back into its cradle. Behind me, the door opened and Lloyd stuck his head in.

"I think it's started," he said, his face white. The phone rang and we both looked at it. I'd forgotten to withhold the number. It rang and filled the house. I'd never heard it do that before.

"Are you going to answer that?" asked Lloyd after six rings. I shook my head. Inside that mouthpiece, everything from before. The hot smoked air, the birds. The salted ends of my hair when it flew in my mouth. My family.

183

I unplugged the phone from the wall and the silence was instant. I rested my rifle over my shoulder, nodded to Lloyd, and we headed back to the shed.

The woolshed was a dark block against the hill. I washed my hands in the trough, while Lloyd went on ahead of me. I could feel it, the ripple going through the sheep, the new feeling for some of them, the old familiar ache for others. The hiss of leaves in the wind and from behind the shed, a single low sheep call. I felt it, the skin on my back prickling like something stared hard at me from behind the dark. It was holding its breath but it was there.

In the doorway I breathed in the manure and warmth and blood of what was happening. I could make out three who were shifting about, unsettled, one who threw her head back, curling her upper lip. Lloyd crouched by her pen and stroked Dog. His beard made it look like a nativity scene. He glanced up at me and shrugged.

"I don't know what I'm supposed to do."

"It's okay," I said, "she knows what to do, she's done it before." Last year she'd had triplets—one girl and two boys. The girl now scraped the ground outside with her hooves, waiting for her turn. The boys had gone with the butcher.

I walked slowly up to her and she stood and turned around, like when Dog makes a nest. Her waterbag poked out of her and as she twisted, it burst and she turned around again, surprised-looking, and licked at the wet spot on the floor.

"What in god's name was that?"

"Her waters," I said.

Lloyd shook his head in disbelief.

"Did you think she'd lay an egg?"

I waited until the head and forelegs were showing and then I

184

checked another two who were shifting. I felt like I could lie down in the hay with them, a pang, just for a moment, of what it must be like to give birth to something, and then I went to get the iodine spray. Soon there would be more of us.

By the time the first lamb slid out, the others were in full swing, the quiet stomp of mothers trying to get comfortable, the dark smell of blood and the wet warmth. I unhooked a shoulder from the umbilical cord with my gloved fingers, and out spilled a boy lamb and then soon after, his sister. The night went on; when there was a lull, when the shed went quiet, Lloyd poured coffee and mixed it with whisky.

"I'm not much use," he said.

"I feel better having you here," I said and blushed because I hadn't expected to say that. He drank his drink and put honey on a slice of bread for me.

"I don't expect your hands are all that clean," he said and he held it up to my mouth. I took a bite even though I wasn't hungry. In the quiet time last year I'd hurried back to the house and slept for a few hours. Now instead, I passed a torch over the sheep left outside. I counted and counted again. I went back to the shed and sat down in the hay next to Lloyd and Dog. We watched the lambs in the orange glow of the gas lamp.

"You got any children?" Lloyd asked.

"No."

"Me neither."

When the first washes of light came up over the fields, I got on to docking and tagging the lambs. Lloyd held them with his hand over their eyes while I did it.

"It's not that bad," I told him, "just like having your ears pierced."

He looked at me. "How would you know?"

The lamb wriggled as I passed the punch through the cartilage.

185

"He's just startled by the noise," I said and moved around Lloyd to get to the tail. I slipped on the band and motioned for the lamb to be put back in the pen. It bumped around trying to get away from the feeling of it chasing him.

By the time we were done a morning breeze had crept into the shed and Lloyd was staring at the void that was his first dead lamb. It had come out grey and frog-like. I put a small triplet under the dead body and we watched while the mother of the dead lamb nosed the body off and started to lick at the nose and mouth of the live one. It let out muffled baas and its tail switched underneath it. I yawned loudly.

"You go and rest," Lloyd said, his voice a croak. "I'll come and get you if anything happens." Dog was settled watching Lloyd watch the dead lamb. My neck ached.

"I'll have a quick bath," I said, "I'll be half an hour."

Crossing the field, for a moment the sky was blue, making the trees black at their trunks. I reached the doorway of my house and looked out. It was still there, whatever it was, the feeling like something had hunkered down in the valley, waiting and watching and ready to stoop.

While the bath filled I sat on the toilet lid, listening to the sound of the sparrows that nested under my bedroom window waking up as the light began to come into the sky.

The water was hotter than I could bear and I couldn't get my hand in deep enough to touch the plug without feeling it start to cook, so I ran the cold. My bones ached like a creaking boat. By the time the water was manageable, I was cold and my feet prickled as I submerged them. As I lowered myself in, the water started to spill onto the floor, and scrabbling for the plug I lost my balance and fell backwards, smacking my head against the back of the bath, and the water formed into two colliding waves, which splashed out and all over the place. It ran through the gaps in the floorboards in a steady stream and would show up as a brown stain on the kitchen ceiling. My head hurt. I kept my eyes closed and breathed out through my mouth, afraid of the moment I would have to assess the damage. Poor Archimedes idiot.

The back door opened downstairs. I opened my eyes. There was some blood. It was not too bad, considering the crack it had made, and the thump I was feeling, but then I saw that actually there was quite a lot, and it was turning the water around my shoulders luminous green. Downstairs, it was Lloyd. It was Lloyd downstairs.

He mounted the stairs. It was nobody else but Lloyd come to give me some news on the sheep. And then Lloyd was pelting up the stairs, faster than his feet could fly, and light, like he had more than one set of legs, and in a second he had beaten a path along the hallway and right into my bedroom, without even knocking, and he was standing right on the other side of the bathroom door, breathing, and I knew that it was not Lloyd. It was something else. Light blocked out in patches underneath the door, it stood perfectly still and panted deep in the back of its throat. I couldn't remember if I had turned the key in the bathroom door or not. I held my breath and the panting stopped. There was a thump on the door, and I splashed more water out of the bath, and a splitting pain slammed through my head.

"Lloyd?" I called. The key in the door trembled but it did not open and whatever was on the other side started running again, pounded once more on the door as it passed it, then ran fast around the bedroom. I heard the springs creak as it flew over the bed, and then it was out of the room, slamming the door behind it, and it carried on up the stairs, up and up the stairs that were not there because there was no room above mine, and then the house was silent, apart from a soft wheezing sound that came from me. The water was cold and I was no longer sure

24

Outside Darwin, I pick rock melons and cucumbers with the spines that stick in my palms and fill with pus at night. Out in the sun, my scars are still tacky and they stick to my T-shirt and remind me they're there. I make about $20 a day, which is enough to eat or sleep but not both, and sleeping in the YHA dormitory is miserable. There are bedbugs and worst of all there are the other sleepers who are all backpackers. They are English or Canadian or Scottish, which I thought was the same as English, but it turns out is very different. They frighten me, these people with their white dreadlocks and their ease at sleeping next to strangers. They think I'm their age because of my height, and one guy invites me out to watch them play drinking games. When I say I haven't got the money, he says he'll shout me one, and then I spend the night watching men have box-wine bladders poured down their throats, and then I watch them wheel off and puke up under the trees I sometimes sleep under.

In the bunks at the YHA I wake up one night, the taste of smoke in my mouth, and my heart is pumping and flapping about inside me. I stay still and wait until my eyes get used to the dark, listening to the different styles of breathing and snoring the other people in the room have. When my eyes become used to the dark, I can see that the guy on the bunk on top of me has his head hung over the side, and he's watching me, not moving, not making a sound, just watching me with eyes that look black and wet in the dark. I shut my eyes and don't move until morning, until I hear the man get down off his bunk and leave.

I put a bit aside every day and have enough to buy a second-hand sleeping bag, and I decide outside alone on the beach with a full belly is better than the YHA with all those creepy people. During the day I stash my bag behind a closed snack bar in an old bread tray. It's hard work fruit-picking, and by the end of a day I'm starving, so it's a good feeling to be able to get a calamari burger and chips and then sit in my bag and watch the fruit bats swoop about. I sleep well on those nights, while it's warm and dry. In the mornings I swim in the sea.

When the season starts to change, there are no more things to pick, and the very little I've saved up gets me each day a dim sum from the fish shop and an apple or an orange. Sometimes the fish-shop guy chucks in some chips, because he says at least I keep myself clean and I don't put his customers off. Which is sort of a nice thing, but it means he thinks I'm a homeless. Which all in all is pretty accurate.

My clothes start to go a bit rancid—I've got three changes which stay in the bottom of my bag, and washing them in sea water doesn't do much of a job. I have to leave my bag sometimes when I go and try and find work. I get a cleaning job, disinfecting the public toilets around town. It makes less than fruit-picking and is longer hours and when I get back to my bag and my clothes, someone's binned the lot and it's all gone.

I lie to the woman who gives me the job, and say I have my own transport, which means I spend most of the day walking around town with a stinking bucket of bleach, and the air sanitiser which is supposed to be peach smelling but which smells of crap as well as of peach. I have to return the mop and bucket by 7 p.m. each day, so sometimes I have to miss cleaning a toilet or two. I know they make spot checks, so every morning I'm terrified of being caught out. I smell awful, it's in my hair and my skin and I'm pretty sure that peach 'n' crap smell comes out on my breath. The fish man stops giving me free chips, and I stop going there because it's embarrassing. I get out in the breakers, which feels dangerous after dark and it's cold now too, and I snort up sea water to try and get the peach out. Up here is the water the whale sharks move through at this time of year, the only sharks people get sad about if one of them gets stuck in a trawler's net or washes up. I think of those big fish and their wide toothless mouths out there and then I think of their smaller cousins with the teeth and I imagine them brushing against my legs.

While I'm making myself comfortable in the wide roots of a mango tree, a man offers me $30 to put his dick in my mouth. It seems like so little to ask for, such a short amount of time to have taken up. He gives me $15 and says, "There, half before and half after," and I feel like I've tricked him. That I have a tongue and a hole in my face means that in four or six minutes I can make more than a whole day of stooped, stinking work in the toilets. He holds the hair at the back of my head and drives his dick in hard so that it chokes me, like he is taking a swab, and his fingers in my hair tighten when he comes. It's all over pretty quickly, the only really bad bit is when I have his stuff in my mouth and I think he might not give me the other half of the money if I look ill, and so I swallow it and give him what I hope is a winning smile. The man smiles back and wipes something from my cheek. He tucks his dick away in his trousers and reaches into his pocket. He gives me another $20 and says, "You get extra for that nice smile." And then he leaves. I buy myself a single room in a YHA, and lie awake most of the night because I feel excited about what the money means, but also because my stomach is churning.

191

25

"At worst," the doctor said, "it's a light concussion. Don't drink, get plenty of rest and you'll be fine."

Lloyd laughed and the doctor looked at him.

"And you shouldn't be alone," he said. "Make sure your husband takes good care of you." He passed a glance around the place, the empty bottles and unwashed dishes.

The silence left after the doctor had gone was heavy. I sat up off the sofa and held my head in my hands. It throbbed but it didn't hurt.

"So what happened? Did you just lose your balance or was it a cry for help? Honestly, when I first came in I thought you'd done yourself in. Imagine how that would look! Strange man shows up and lures unsuspecting spinster to her death."

"Something was in the house."

Lloyd looked at me, smiling.

"Something?"

"It was the thing that's being doing the stuff."

Lloyd frowned. "The thing that's been doing the stuff?"

I pointed out the window. "I heard it, it came into the house, up the stairs, it jumped on my bed. I thought it was you but it wasn't."

"Well, I had Dog with me."

"It wasn't a dog. It wasn't human."

"Neither is a dog."

"I think it was not from . . . around here." Lloyd's eyes narrowed. He opened his mouth and closed it.

"Look—you've got a concussion."

"Things have been happening here," I said, and there was a wobble in my throat.

"I understand that—I imagine this is a stressful season for a farmer—"

"I'm not a hysterical woman."

"No, but it doesn't help anyone if you start deciding there are monsters in the woods. This is a wild place, there could be all sorts of animals you don't know about—"

"I know about all of the animals." My face was red and hot and suddenly I was very embarrassed. Lloyd had his back to me, and the room was tense.

"You saw me naked," I said, to break the atmosphere. "How was that?"

Lloyd looked at me and I waited. "Like all my nightmares come at once. You're not supposed to drink," he said, pouring me a glass of whisky.

"And I'm supposed to rest."

He handed me the glass. "You're not leaving me alone with those sheep."

I stood, testing my balance and touching the bandage that was wrapped around the top of my head. "I feel fine."

"You look mad," Lloyd said and drained his drink.

Lloyd limed the empty pens while I tubed paste into the new lambs.

"What's next?" he asked; the visible parts of his face between his hat and his beard were flushed.

"We just keep watching," I said.

"How long before they go to market?"

"Shhh," I said and turned away. "When they're ready." There was a long silence, just the noises of Lloyd raking out the pens and the occasional bleat from an occupied stall.

One ewe with triplets was not interested in the smallest one. It struggled to get close to her and got squashed out by the other two. After a while it settled itself down on its own and cried. I picked her up and she didn't struggle, wrapped her in a blanket and gave her to Lloyd to hold while I made a bottle ready. "Not sure she'll make it," I told him.

"Why is this all so sad?" he asked. He stroked the bony head and the lamb nuzzled against his jumper looking for a teat.

Back at the house, we wrapped the lamb in a blanket and put it in front of the stove on Dog's bed, and locked Dog in Lloyd's room. I set the timer on the stove so we'd wake to feed her, and Lloyd went into the sitting room and made a fire. We sat on the sofa watching the flames.

There was just the hollow ticking of the kitchen clock. My head itched underneath the bandage, but there was no energy left in my arm to scratch it.

A knock at the door.

Don stood behind Samson, who had had a wash since I last saw him. Then Marcie stepped out of the dark, holding her arms around herself and looking embarrassed.

"Caught these two out by the woolshed," Don said.

"Doing what?"

"Pissing about." Don's face was hard. He gave Samson a small shove in the back and Samson stumbled over the threshold. Marcie followed and Don closed the door behind them.

"What were you doing?" I said turning to Samson. He looked at the floor.

"We were just looking at the lambs, that's all," Marcie said.

195

"Did you hurt any of them?"

"No!" She sounded upset, but Samson was just quiet.

"He had firelighters on him and matches," said Don. There was a slight swelling on Samson's face, a redness about his eye like he'd been hit.

"We were just—"

Don interrupted Marcie. "Shut your trap, I don't want to hear it."

"Please don't tell my dad," she said quietly and started to cry. Samson moved his hand across to her and held on to her little finger. All of us watched that.

"Samson," I said quietly, "what were you doing up there—what were you going to do with those firelighters?"

He looked up and I saw suddenly Don's old face in his, and I felt sad.

"We were just up there to watch over them. That's all. Was going to make a fire—outside—to sit around, and just watch them. Keep them safe."

"Safe from what?" asked Lloyd, but Samson didn't reply, just chewed his lips and looked at me, held my gaze until Don chafed him on the back of the head.

"Well, answer him," he muttered.

"It's okay, Don," I said. Marcie sniffed and wiped her nose on the back of her hand. Mascara muddied the whites of her eyes. "No harm done."

Once they'd gone, Don marching them out, telling Marcie she was getting driven back home and a word in the ear of her parents, Samson all the while gripping on to her little finger, we sat down at the table.

"God almighty, what do you think they were going to do?" Lloyd said.

"I think they were going to start a small fire to keep warm and sit around it and watch over my sheep. I think they might have smoked cigarettes and drunk beer and had a pash."

"You've changed your tune. What happened to the kids chopping up your sheep?"

"I think Samson's seen it."

"Seen what?"

"The thing out there that's getting the sheep."

"The fox?"

"It's not a fox."

There was a long silence.

"I get the feeling," said Lloyd, "that you're very tired."

The buzzer on the stove sounded.

26

Flora Carter's memorial service is attended by everyone in the town other than her father. We fill up the jetty, and I imagine it creaking and then collapsing, throwing all of us into the water. Hay Carter stands alone, with space around her, and all I can think is that I've never seen her in black before. Only cut-offs and white singlets with the bra straps showing. Today nothing shows, she is swallowed by the black dress, bodyless, just her feet poke out the bottom, heels that she will struggle to walk back down the jetty in, that will stick in the cracks of the soft sun-bleached wood.

People say different things about Flora. Someone sings the song from the *Titanic* movie. The triplets fidget next to me, whisper to one another and then Iris smacks one of them on the back of the head and they are quiet again. I don't hear any words, but I do hear the splash of the wreath as it's thrown into the water. I see Denver's mother is watching from the edge of the trees. I think we look each other in the eye. She takes three slow steps backwards into the shrub and she stands still. *The human eye senses movement before all else.*

Back home, Mum pours a glass of wine, does nothing about making lunch for the triplets who bang through the cupboards, looking for food. Iris is already upstairs, out of the way of us all. I perch at the kitchen table with Mum, and Dad opens a beer and stands with his back to us.

"That kid ever wakes up," he says, "he's in for a helluva shock." I look up at him, his fists on his hips and his hat low over his eyes. "Steve Warren says they've put round-the-clock security at his bedside—reckon people might get ideas." He turns around and looks at us, swigs his beer. "Reckon they might have the right idea." Mum looks up sharply.

"John! Don't say things like that."

"If that was my daughter, dead in the ground, it'd take more than a couple of cops to stop me getting to the little hoon." When he says the word "daughter" my father rests his hands on my shoulders.

"Don't swear in front of the children."

"Hoon?"

"They don't know he did it," I say quietly. Mum and Dad stop arguing and both look at me.

"Jake. Don't you get all lefty here—they found him over where the fire started, reckon he was after Flora all along. Who knows what he did to her before he started the fire. Covering his tracks more than likely."

"He wouldn't do that."

"You don't know anything," Mum snaps in a way that seems to surprise her, and she stands up, leaving her wine, to get on with the laundry.

From what I have heard about comas, they reckon you can still hear, even if you can't move. I wonder if Denver lies there listening to all these people talking about what will happen to him if he wakes up and if it will make him decide to die instead.

I follow the burnt trail down to the beach, but I go the long way round so I don't pass the spot I last saw Denver. I stop when I come across a wombat, swollen and on its back. He looks like someone has taken a blowtorch to him, all his hair is missing, and his skin is flaky charcoal. He looks like he would pop if I nudged him with my foot. I nudge him with my foot and he doesn't. There's still a smell to the bush, like it's thinking it might go up again, and I know I'm not supposed to be there. The trees don't want me there, they are black stakes and behind lots of them are small piles of ashes that could be the remains of animals sheltering. There is not a single bird to make sound, not a cicada or a cricket, not even a mosquito to whine at my ear. Down by the sea, there's a blackness to the water and to the beach, ash rolls in the waves and dead birds have washed up out of it. Flies are the only things that have made any headway out of this, and they rise in flocks when I walk by the bodies that must have dropped out of the air. Some of them are perfect, a kookaburra, a honeyeater, a bowerbird.

You're not supposed to swim this time of year because the whalers come in close to feed on the mackerel. I drag the boat out to the water and it makes grooves in the sand, and I think that might be the last they'll know of me, deep large footprints in the sand and the surprising strength of a fifteen-year-old girl. I row until I'm just past the reef, and I drop the small anchor, feel it catch and the boat turns in a circle. No one can see me out here, so I take my T-shirt off. I fix myself up with the goggles, which make my eyes bulge because they're too small, and I fix the snorkel to the side of my face, bite down on it. I sit lightly on the side of the boat like scuba divers do, thinking I'll go in backwards, but the boat nearly capsizes, so in the end I just jump out like a mad kid. The water is warm and clear. Butterfish scoot in and out between each other. I dive down to the sea floor. It is not deep, not deep deep black blue which would be frightening. The seabed is soft and sandy, and when I feel it with the flat of my palm, white sand billows up, sparkling gold and silver and floating like dust motes in the small swell. Prawns with long moustaches walk the water around me and I look up and see a flock of birds so clearly my goggles fog. The sharks fly with the urgency of ice melting. There is no thrash, no gums bared and raw-meat teeth, no rolling eyes and fat green blood-cloud. I have only a few moments before I have to go up for air, have to rise up between them, but I don't move for what feels like the longest time, not until my eyes feel like they might start to bleed from the pressure. One bubble at a time I let my breath out. They feed in this quiet way, occasionally darting forward a few feet to swallow a small fish, barely opening their wide mouths, sucking soup from a spoon. They sing to each other—it is just the pressure in my ears, the sound of needing to breathe, of course it is, but I can hear a high-pitched ticking, a noise like air let slowly out of a balloon, and I imagine it's their song. When the last air bubble has left my mouth, I let myself float to the surface, coming face-to-face with a dozen of them, and they do not care, they don't want me, and only turn in a tight circle when I put out my hand to touch them, turn in a tight circle and fly away. When I break the surface, I breathe in and in and out again, and there's a sharp pain at my temple, and black spots appear and then disappear from my eyes. It's now, looking down, that I feel uneasy, and I see how far I have gone from the boat in coming up, not keeping my eye on its shadow, and I lap across the top, with those great birds underneath me, watching me like I have watched them, hearing the beat of my heart, the mess I make of the top of the water. One of them brushes gently against my foot, but it doesn't bite, there is just, when I pull myself into the boat, the smallest of grazes, and I lie in the bottom of the boat, jumping with sea lice, feeling them moving underneath me, and I get the feeling that nothing matters all that much any more. When I close my eyes, I see smoke-blackened people

legs. The man's eyes fall on the grapes. "He can't swallow, love," he says. "He won't be swallowing down anything any more—the throat is gone."

How can a person's throat be gone? I think—it must be a figure of speech. How would the head connect?

"Reckon he's got his own punishment being left in a state like that—no eyelids, no lips. Not enough skin to see him through the grafts."

Lead weight gathers in my belly. "Please," I say. I'm not sure what it is I'm pleading for, but it has some effect on the man. He squints at me.

"You're John Whyte's daughter." I nod and he sighs. "Look, I'm going to assume you're as good a bloke as your old man. I've got the toilet to use, while I'm gone you can do what you like, just don't touch him." He picks up a paper he's been sitting on. "Leave those grapes outside, and remember—I know exactly who you are." He puts his thumbs into the space between his stomach and belt, "And if a nurse comes in, I didn't see you."

I put the grapes down on his empty seat. "Thanks," I say.

He walks away, his shoes squeaking on the floor. I open the door to Denver's room, where he is encased in a plastic cover, like a small tent. There's a smell in the room, at the same time familiar and so alien that the breath stops in my throat—the deep-fat fryer.

A machine pumps air into the body inside the plastic. The sound is calm and regular, a steady wheeze. I can only catch glimpses of Denver's body, dark patches of pink between white bandages. If he is awake I wonder what he knows, this new order of things, no arms or legs to use, just flesh, cooking while he sits inside it and stares at the ceiling through the tent. My mouth is bone-dry. There's the smallest sound from the tent, like a squeal, the noise of fat spitting in a pan. The thing under plastic lives, and I wipe my palms on my thighs and move closer.

"Denver?" I am waiting for an answer that won't come. "It's Jake." Somewhere a series of beeps sound. The pump feeds him air. "I've come to say I'm sorry." I move closer and try not to look at his face. His eyes are covered over with pads of cotton, so he cannot even stare at the ceiling, but I am glad not to have to meet the gaze of the eyeballs. In the moist cave of his mouth is a thick plastic tube. It is impossible to tell which of the other tubes carry urine or pus or drugs, all of them are Dettol-brown. I breathe in through my mouth to avoid the smell, but I still get the taste.

"I don't know if you can hear me," I say like they do on the TV. "I just wanted to say that I didn't mean for this to happen." I leave a long pause like he might respond. I can't remember any more what it is that I expected to happen. "And I want you to know that if you wake up, I'll tell them it was me, I won't let them hurt you." It had sounded so heroic when I'd practised it in my head. But in my head, Denver was still a complete body, maybe with a few scars about him, maybe even an oxygen mask over his face for the smoke inhalation. He was not this wet wound of meat. "I'm so sorry," I say again. "It's all my fault, I never thought it would get so out of control. The fire—"

"How do you mean it's all your fault?" Behind me, at the open doorway, stands a nurse and the policeman. I push past them and into the hallway.

"Hey," the policeman calls, but he doesn't follow me. I look back and they are both just standing looking.

"Who is that?" the nurse asks the policeman.

"I know her old man," he says.

For an hour I walk the blackened main street, and people turn to look at me, in a way that I can't read. I try to smile back at some of them, some sympathetic sort of smile that would be appropriate,

204

but they turn away if I do that. There's a silence of so many people looking. No one asks questions. No one says anything, they just look and all of them see me. And all of them look that quiet look.

The post office, the pub and the co-op are fine, but the fish shop is dead, and outside it I can see the fish man sitting on the bonnet of his car and just looking. There's no one there to help him because everyone is looking to their own problems. He must sense me watching because he looks up, and he just stares at me. I put my hands deep in the pockets of my shorts and keep my head down. I think I hear him shout something, but probably not, probably no one heard. I don't look behind me, I turn down the street that takes me back down towards the beach. Somewhere I hear the scratch of a walkie-talkie, I hear my name on the wind.

I take myself far far away from what I am worried about, I think only about how I will sit for a while on the beach, and then I will go home and at home I will go to sleep and in the morning I will start to think straight again, I will wake up a changed and better person and I will be able to think clearly about the past week, about Flora, about Denver, their parents and the town. I walk quickly and soon, in the baking heat, I am on the beach again, the place with the reedy dunes where the soldier crabs pop their heads out of their holes and tick their moustaches at you, but today, no matter how still I sit, no faces appear out of the sand. There is nothing to be frightened away by a flung-out hand, nothing will be conducted in the way that it should be, and I am still not thinking clearly.

I hear twigs snap behind me and I ignore it. Up the beach come six or seven men and a woman. I don't move. The human eye. If I move, where will I end up? If I move I'm guilty. And I stay put until I can see who they are, walking with a purpose, all of them. One man is Andy Carter and my blood bellows in my stomach. The woman runs the bread shop. I have a memory of her when I was younger, giving out the stale iced buns to kids on their way home from school. The fish man is with them, with the same look he'd given me half an hour before. The other faces I recognise but not enough to name—I have never been interested enough in learning these people's names. I keep still, like a leveret; my shorts are sand-coloured, my T-shirt green, they will not see me if I remain still. But I catch in Andy Carter's face that he has seen me, and I wait a breath to try to work out a plan and at the last moment, I get up and run. There is a shout behind me, a scream from the bread-shop woman and through the earth I feel them coming. If I can make it round the headland, I can hide until I can take my boat and get away. I am a fast runner for my year, I am tall and long-legged.

Someone tackles me to the ground and the wind is knocked out of me, and there is not enough air in me to say I'm sorry, it was an accident, there is just a cronking sound that comes from my chest, and my T-shirt is being pulled over my head, my arms and legs are pinned by the weight of bodies and there is a sudden scalding-hot pain, the sound of yelling and waves and the steady bleat of my own voice above the sound of a stick whistling through the air and being brought down again and again on my back. I flip like an eel in the sand, and see Andy Carter, his face a red crease of fury, and I see the fish man with his face less certain, but the fish man says, "Let him take his turn and then we'll get you home." The bread lady looks away from it all and out to sea with her hands on top of her head, and I am tossed back onto my stomach by the fish man and the other nameless men and the blows come again and each time I feel flesh being torn and I am a wet bag of meat like Denver, torn and open and not human any more. My hand digs into the sand to hide itself, it is like the pink claw of a galah.

From down the beach, there is someone else's scream, a burning-hot scream, and the stick stops and there is just enough air in my lungs that I can make the smallest of screeches when I breathe out. My face presses against the ground and through one eye I see four bodies on top of Andy Carter, holding him down and making him stop. A ringing in my ears like the birds, a squalling in my chest.

27

I woke up with a jolt and Dog was standing at the foot of my bed, ears pricked. It sounded like a dog fight out in the bottom field. There was nothing to see out the fogged window. I opened it, took the torch from my bedside table and shone it out there. A scream of something and the beam caught the black shape, just for a second, and the sheep, white blurs in the top corner of the field, huddled. The noise was still there, guttural, and the sheep called out.

"Jesus fuck." I pulled jeans on over my nightshirt. Dog stayed still, his eyes wide, tail straight out behind him. I grabbed the gun from the cupboard and banged the bedroom door closed behind me so Dog wouldn't follow, flew down the stairs and smashed my palm flat against Lloyd's bedroom door twice before I got to the front door and crammed my feet into my boots. I heard Dog scratching and barking upstairs and the sound of Lloyd opening his door, and then I was gone into the dark, running blind.

I'd put down the torch when I'd picked up the gun, but I would shoot whatever came at me, whatever it was that was snapping and slobbering in the dark. I held my gun out in front of me in case I ran smack into a tree, and by the time I made it to the fence, I could see the shape darting around the huddle of sheep who were crying now and who were far away from me, still, and the shape was taller and wider than a man, but it disappeared when I tried to aim, when I looked too hard at it. The noise kept me on it, kept me following, a panting, a deep mucus sound with a whine at either end of it. For a second, I had it in my sights, and I understood what I was looking at, thought it had turned to look at me too, and then I fired and the sheep scattered. The sound of birds taking flight from the woods. I heard my name being called, and Dog shrilling at my bedroom window—my head throbbed hard enough that I sat right down in the wet grass and pressed it into the ground.

A torch beam wobbled from far off, and I saw the Christmas colours, the green grass and white wool, a smear of red, the steam rising.

Lloyd was a hand on my shoulder. "Are you hurt?" he said, and I sat up and wiped my eyes, then covered them over with my hands.

"I shot something," I said though there was barely enough air to say it.

He picked up my gun and took himself up the field. Between the crying of the sheep and the whinnying of Dog in the bedroom came a shot.

I heard Lloyd tramp back across the field and started to feel the cold dew against the heat of blood. When he shone it at me his torch took away any night vision I had, I couldn't see his face, but I could tell from his breathing, like something an old dog would make, that he had done something he didn't like.

"It was a sheep. In the neck. I finished her off." He cocked the gun, tipped the cartridges out into his hand and pocketed them like he'd done it before.

28

I keep my back to the fire and walk slowly. It races along the edge of town. The door of the post office is open and no one's inside. At the pub they have thought to close their doors; I can imagine someone getting in there and drinking the barrels dry while the world burns around them. The smell is of barbecue and eucalyptus and the sound is a roar that will crush everything.

The main street is empty apart from smoke, coddled so thick that I can't see to the end where the road forks away from the fish shop and up towards home. A pademelon hops out from behind a parked car and we look at each other. Her ears are flat to her head, her eyes beady and bright. She sneezes and whips back underneath the car. There come more and more animals—a wallaby, sheltering from hot ashes in the bakery's doorway, snakes whip into the road to collect in the gutter. A goanna stands still, watches me go by. Behind the shops at the end of town I can see the fire has made its way round, and looking back down the main street from where I've come, a kangaroo jumps, panicked, across the road away from a spot-fire that's started up there, on the bitumen where nothing should burn. There's a roar in the air. People talk about the roar a shark makes when it comes for you, the monster noise of it, hungry for your flesh and bones.

By the time I reach home, my arms are black with soot and my eyes are running. There's a metal button on my shorts which burns into my thigh, and my plastic wristwatch has become soft. There is no one home. Someone has had the hose on and doused the dead grass at the front of the house, and sprayed the walls. The hose still runs. I sit on the front steps and ash is falling all around. Spot-fires, jumping devils, break away from the central roar. This is my home, I think, this is where nothing can get me. I'm not breathing air any more and so I go inside. Once the fly-screen has banged shut, my pulse starts to race. I feel aware for the first time of what is happening. I try to remember the fire classes at school, and I get the towels and sheets out of the cupboard that Mum folds them into, plug and run the bath and throw them in. Downstairs I turn on the kitchen tap, start to fill up the mop bucket, and then I collect the wet towels from the bath, and stuff them under the front door. The sheets I hang over the windows, and I keep one to wrap myself in. The water has stopped running into the mop bucket, there's just a soft trickle now, so that's it, that's my water. While I'm thinking, a tree falls nearby, and it sounds like something is smashing its way through the bush towards me.

I open the freezer and there are two bags of ice in there for Mum's daiquiris, and some block coolers for picnics. I take them out but I'm not sure what to do with them. I move the towel from underneath the front door and open it, thinking I will scatter the ice over the veranda, but outside everything is black, like the dead part of the night. Above me, where there should be sky, I see a redness and the ice in my arms starts to melt, like I'm holding it under a hot tap. My eyes hurt, and I smell burning hair so I close the door and stuff the towel back under it, put the melting ice back in the freezer and go to the triplets' room with the mop bucket which is only half filled. Their room has a small window that opens onto the roof and has been nailed shut to stop them going out there and falling off. I can already see embers settling

211

29

Lloyd gripped me around the waist and helped me up, and just as I was about to complain that I could do it myself, I felt that I couldn't.

"The body," I said.

"I'll sort it."

I sat in the kitchen drinking hot water and listened to the sounds of him with the wheelbarrow, into the field, out again. Dog curled himself around my feet and shook and I fondled his ears.

"Sorry, love," I said to him quietly. "I'm sorry."

Lloyd came back in.

"Listen," I said, "I want to bring the sheep inside."

"In where?" he said, sitting carefully down opposite me—I wondered if he had given himself a bad back.

"In here. Just for now, until we find it."

"In here—in your house?"

"Yes—just until we find the thing. It's getting bolder."

Lloyd looked at me for a long time.

"This is your house," he said, "and those are your sheep. But I'm not going to let you do that."

"I've got to protect them somehow," I said, but even as I said it I felt like I wouldn't win, that I wouldn't be able to do it without him. I thought of the sheep I shot in the neck and put my head on the table. Dog rested his chin on my knee and Lloyd poured us both a whisky but I pushed mine away.

Something nested outside the window, and it sang loudly, *Chip, chjjjj, chewk, jaay and jaay-jaay, tool-ool, tweedle-dee, chi-chuwee.* It should have been me that finished her, she should have died thinking it was all going to be fine. *Tool-ool, tweedle-dee, chi-chuwee.* I wondered if the other ewes knew it was me.

"Coffee then?" Lloyd said.

He made a pot and took it to the kitchen table and there was a small spillage, just a splash. He got two mugs. He placed the sugar on the table with a spoon and sat down.

"Do you think I'm mad?" I asked. The question wasn't answered, instead Lloyd stretched over and put his hand over mine for a moment. Then he put three spoonfuls of sugar in a mug and poured coffee into it, stirred and passed it to me. I had to hold on to it with both hands because of the shake in my arms.

"Where's the lamb?" I asked, looking at the empty dog bed by the stove. We both listened but there was no other sound from the house.

30

I'm stealing looks at Denver Cobby, the half-Aboriginal kid from the year above. He is outside the gates, smoking and talking with another boy. He doesn't care that anyone can see him, and because of that the teachers don't ever hassle him. He's that cool. I'm pretending to be really into the pebble I'm thumbing, like it's an interesting one or a fossil or something, when Hannah and Nerrida come up to me and start going on.

"How's it going, homo?" Nerrida asks, and I don't look up. They might go away if I ignore them.

"Hey!" Hannah barks. "We're talking to you." And I pretend that I've found something far more interesting than them on my stone. Hannah flicks her hair over to the other side of her head. "Rude bitch," she says. "Your sister's stuck up too—but at least she's fuckin' got a pair of balls."

Nerrida shoves my arm, and my stone drops between my knees and bounces onto the floor. Now I have nothing to train my attention to. I've seen Nerrida go for girls before, her older sister has a scar on her cheek where Nerrida dug her nails in one time.

"Look at me when I'm talking to you," she says and she grabs my face in her claws and yanks it round so I'm looking at her. "Fucking dyke," she says, and someone shouts, "You girls, leave her the fuck alone," and they both turn around with looks on their faces like someone's going to die, but then they see it's Flora Carter that's spoken, and Nerrida drops her hand from my face.

"We were just playin' with her," Hannah complains, but Flora points to the other side of the yard and they start to leave without saying anything apart from Nerrida who mumbles "Sorry" as she passes Flora.

Flora Carter picks up the stone I was holding and passes it back to me. "You all right?" she asks, and I'm bright red in the face. Over her shoulder I can see that Denver is looking.

After school, I'm supposed to be waiting for Iris, but she hasn't shown. Bad things always happen when you're waiting for Iris.

"I fucked your dad last night," says Nerrida outside the gates. "How'd you like me as a stepmum?" Hannah is having hysterics behind Nerrida, wiping tears from her eyes. I pull my shoulders into my body, try and become small and I look away from them both. "Don't worry," she carries on, "I wouldn't marry him—his dick's like that." She holds up her little finger and wiggles it at me. I'm offended on Dad's behalf.

"Reckon you've got a bigger dick than your dad," Hannah pipes up, which sets them both off, but Nerrida recovers quickly, in time to get close enough for me to smell her breath of raspberry Icy Pole.

"Have you got a big dick, Brick Shit House?" I've waited for Iris long enough, and I turn to walk away, but Nerrida grabs my arm and yanks me back round. "When will you learn to be respectful to your elders?" she shrills like a mum, not my mum but one of the ones that comes out of the church.

"Hey. You want me to walk you home?" Denver Cobby has appeared next to me. I can feel the heat of his blood through his arm, even though it's not touching mine. Hannah smiles and blushes a little.

"That'd be nice, sure," she says. There's a pause.

Denver snorts, "Not you," and Nerrida looks up, a smile just about to form on her lips when Denver puts his hot arm around my waist. I try not to jump. As he walks me away I hear Nerrida say, "What the fuck?" and it is the most triumphant moment of my life, even though I will pay for it tomorrow.

Denver walks me to the end of our drive—he's talked the whole way about his favourite footy stars, and I don't mind because I can't think of anything to say back, just enjoy that he is talking to me. I wish Iris was here to see, I wish someone had passed us on the road home, to stop and think, *That Whyte girl's making friends in interesting places.*

"Anyway," he says, a whip of a smile on his lips, like he wants to ask me something but can't bring himself to. "Ignore Nerrida, she's a skank. I can walk you home tomorrow. If you want." And he's off again, but he treads off the path, goes into the bush and disappears. It's what Mum would call the Magic of the Abos. I'm still standing there looking at the spot he was in, when he reappears. He sees me watching and waves. "Just having a piss!" he calls, and carries on down the road.

The next morning, I dress carefully. Iris has a new netball skirt I think about thieving, but I wouldn't make it out the door with my eyeballs in my head. Instead I pinch a padded bra from her dirty clothes basket, and I roll my cut-offs up a notch. I have a checked shirt and I experiment with tying it at my navel like Nerrida does. In the end I decide it's better hanging loose—it disguises the strange high shape of the bra. I brush my hair which is not normally something I get round to. With a bit of lipstick I look all right I reckon. There's nothing to be done about my plimsolls, which stink if you get too close. I wonder for the first time about getting a job like Iris has at the Gladioli Tea Shop so I could buy the sandals and nail polish she gets hold of. I think for a second about taking her sandals in my bag, shudder at what she'd do to me when she found out. The bra is a big enough risk.

I am proud of my new string bikini from Target. "You'll look like a hooker," Mum'd said, but she gave in because at least it was on special. I wonder about wearing it over the top of the padded bra—if it comes to swimming, that bridge will have to be crossed.

At school, no one comments on the new look, which I take as a sign I have it exactly right. Nerrida gets me in the toilets, just her on her own without Hannah. She gets me by the wrist and digs her nails in. She's just put more scented lip gloss on, and so her lips are very wet and they smell of plastic oranges. It's like being in a snake's mouth, having her claws around my wrist—the more I try and pull away, the deeper into my wrist the nails go.

"Listen, you little bastard," she says, and she's got that church-mum tone to her voice again, and with the other hand she holds up a finger to shake at me. "You need to know that you are fucking dead." She pulls me closer so that our foreheads are almost touching. "Did you hear what I said, were you paying attention, you massive fucking ape? I'm going to kill you." She lets go of my wrist and you can hear the sound of her nails unplugging from my skin. She loves him too, I think. But it's me he picks up after class.

It's so hot I have to take my shirt off and tie it round my waist, which ruins the new length of my cut-offs and shows the odd lumps of my bra through my singlet, but it's not all bad. The route we take through the bush has a narrow pathway and I lead the way, looking back over my shoulder now and again to check he's still following. I get the feeling he's more into legs anyway. I hold a whip of wait-a-while out of his way so that it doesn't spring back and catch him. "You're a good bloke, Jake," Denver says with a smile around his voice, in a way that I'm pretty sure says he doesn't really think I am a bloke at all. And then we go to silence, just the crust of us walking, me tootling around with a stick, looking for things to draw his attention to, and enjoying the feel of his eyes on my legs. Probably he'll want to take me out, maybe I'll meet his parents—his younger brother I've seen running a stick down the beach at low tide, maybe I'll become a sort of older-sister figure to him. I have experience of that, I can make Anzacs and the whole lot of them would want me round all the time. Or maybe his parents will disapprove, maybe they'll think I'm too young, or they don't want their son going out with a whitey. We'll ride out of town on his dirt bike, me clutching around his waist, or him hanging on to me like I might slip from his grasp.

"Feel like a swim?" he says, wiping sweat from under his eyes.

"Yeah," I say, "I can show you the boat I found," and suddenly it's all panning out, is there a more perfect way of getting kissed than lying in the bottom of a tin boat in the middle of the sea. The stories we will tell our kids. Denver grins at me, and says, "I'd like that."

A curlew and the black tops of the gums against the white sky. Leaves that are brown, grey and blue, crisp with heat, the dry, face-burning heat and eucalypt that empties my nose and there's Denver two steps behind me and we're walking home again. I can feel his eyes on the backs of my calves, which are biscuit-brown with tiny white hairs that catch the sand in them. I have never felt beautiful until this moment, when I know he is watching, when I know he doesn't see me as Jake the Flake, Brick Shit House, the Whopper. I can feel him thinking about touching my legs which now I look at them are long, not thick trunks, but strong and capable. He isn't talking any more—we have been passing back and forth about the football season just gone, I've sensed that I have impressed him because today I said James

Flannery was past his passing peak and that while Kale Aidie was fast, he was a pussy in the tackle. He laughed when I said that, and it was a nice laugh, surprised.

Even the spiders' webs have disintegrated in the heat, burnt away, poof, in the air.

We're on the track down to the beach when he points at the Carters' property and says, "You know, that's Flora's place." Like it would be something I wasn't aware of. I know where we are, know this stretch of bushland like the back of my hand, he doesn't have to tell me where we are. Just round the back of the Carter property there is a sand track that gets you down to the rocks and in the rocks there are things to look at and to talk about. Octopus, nudibranchs, sand sifters, crabs and urchins. Oysters you can prize off with a knife that taste of seawater and cream. I think about the boat I found a month ago in the dunes, and us lying in the bottom feeling the swimmers underneath us. I've got a stolen joint and matches from Iris's hiding place which I know all about. She's going to skin me when she finds out but it'll be worth it. I'd thought that we could smoke it once we were past the main street and into the trees on the way to my house, but the boat is so much better. I wonder at how impressed he will be when I present it to him.

"Listen," says Denver, "you talk with Flora, don'tcha?"

"I do. Sometimes." I pick up the pace a little because it is very hot and a cool breeze would be nice.

"She's nice isn't she?"

"I like her just fine." Although truth be told right now I do not like her fine at all.

"What about me? You like me?" he asks. I go red-hot in the face, but it makes me smile the way he says it, like he's nervous I might say no, as if it were a possible thing to not like Denver Cobby with his hairy legs and his black eyes.

"Yer orright. S'pose." I turn and give him a smile that says, *Yeah—I think you're good.*

"Well look—can you keep a secret?" My heart is blood-thumping in my throat. We can see the back of the Carter house now, through the pigface and jarrah. A shadow passes in front of the window, but we are too far off to see who it is. Denver lets out a sigh that is long and deep.

"Look. Me 'n' Flo—"

Flo?

Flo away and into the sea.

"Me 'n' Flo have been going together the past few months. Only her old man's not all right with that sort of carry-on."

Carrion.

"He won't let blokes near his house, especially not a black bloke. But she's really something, y'know, Jake?" He says my name and I turn to look at him. I think nothing. It doesn't get the chance to get in one ear hole and out the other, I don't let it in. "I'm just about going fucking crazy out here—the two of us are. We're gonna take the bike and head to Cairns. Get a little place there—I've got a mate who reckons he knows a guy with some labouring work I can get into. I dunno, mate, sounds crazy, I know. My fuck!" And he goes on and on, but it is like the tops of my ears fold over and stuff up the holes. Something buzzes past my face, close enough that I can feel the air of its wings vibrate against my eyes. Then my ears open up in time to hear him going on: "But listen, we need someone on our side, try and help us get ourselves together—could you maybe store a bit of stuff at your house for us? Flo's dad runs checks of her room, in case she's hiding smokes or condoms or uh, I dunno, fuckin' comic books, the way he goes on. I sleep on the sofa at Mum's so there's nowhere to put stuff. Thought maybe you had a bed we can stash shit under till we go? Maybe you

221

might be able to lend us a bit of cash if you've got any saved? We need all we can get."

"Do you want to smoke this joint?" I am holding it out in my fist like a lolly. A small frown goes over Denver's lovely face.

"Nah—not a real good idea I wouldn't say."

I hold the thing to my lips. Denver watches me, looking unsure all of a sudden. Good, I think. You should feel unsure.

"So what do you say?" he asks, leaning back a bit with his thumbs in the waistband of his pants. I light the joint. It smoulders red at the tip, and the smoke goes straight into my eye, but I don't let myself blink it out. I watch him standing there, looking like all the world rested on me stashing a sleeping bag under my bed.

"Jake?"

"Go away," I say quietly, and inhale. I've done it before, so if he is expecting me to choke like the kids on TV do, then he is sorely disappointed. I pretend I am Nerrida at the side of the boat sheds, jutting one hip out and crossing one arm over my chest so that I can rest my other elbow on it, keeping the joint near my lips and pretending to pull a hair of tobacco from my mouth. I see for the first time that I am taller than Denver, and I look down my beak nose at him. Jake the Flake the Dyke. The smoke comes out of me, white. Denver runs his hands through his hair.

"Well? Whad'ya say? Say something."

Perhaps he is impressed by how I smoke, I don't know. It looks like it just pisses him off.

"Fuck. What's your problem? Thought we were mates?"

He is shaking his head. I've made him angry.

"Fine then," he says, to my silence. "If you're gonna be shitful about it, fine. I was only walking you home because Flo felt sorry for you. I find you've told anyone, you'll get the beating of your life."

He holds up a finger, and I believe that he means it, but I keep still. I smoke.

"And for Christ's sake, put that out."

When he says that I take the joint from my lips and hold it between the tips of my index finger and thumb. Then I let it drop, foaming red-hot at the tip and it lands with a pat in among the dry crackled leaves on the ground. Denver moves like a snake, stamps the red out and then turns and pushes me so that I fall on the floor. "What in the name of fuck are you doing, stupid bitch? You're as fucking nuts as your whole fucking family."

His face is curled in the wrong places. *Ha*, I think—*not so pretty after all*. He holds up his finger at me like the way you would at a kid or a dog.

"I mean it—you breathe a word of this to anyone . . ." His finger is trembling. "Fuck off home. You can forget we were ever mates, stupid fucking kid." And he glances at the back of the Carter house, looking for some sign of who it is that is at home. There is blond hair on the veranda, I see it as I crane my neck, she is on the rope-swing her father had made her when she was a little kid. Flo into the sea, and away.

Denver is off at a trot, disappearing around the bend where the track leads down to the rocks. No doubt they have a meeting time, no doubt he has known all along that this is where we would come and he can see Flo right after he's sorted out where they'll stash all their stinking rubbish for the journey ahead. They'll be down on those rocks eating the oysters. They'll push the boat down to the sea and they'll float there, lying in the bottom of the hull. It is their boat, I realise, it is there for them, not for me. I can't imagine Flora Carter letting Denver feel up her tits in the bottom of the boat, but what do I know. Not very much.

I am looking at my tree-trunk legs splaying out on the ground where Denver has pushed me. The birds are loud and all singing at once, *Cuk . . . cuk . . . cuk . . . cuk . . . cuk . . . cuk, Hoo-hoo-hoo-hoo-hoo hoooo-hoooo, Wup wup wup wup, Quit-quit-quit.* Near my foot is the stamped-out joint and I reach for it. It is a little ripped and flat, but it still lights, and I smoke while I look up at the white sky with those fingers of blue gum, dark against the space. The birds sound faster and sharper, *Cheerily, cheeriup, cheerio, cheeriup, Chicka-dee-dee-dee-dee, Fee-beee, Cheer, cheer, cheerful, charmer, Tur-a-lee, Purdy purdy purdy . . . Whoit, whoit, whoit, whoit.*

I put the red end of my joint to a leaf and it eats it up with no flame, just like someone has taken the leaf out of existence, like it was never there in the first place. In my head starts a countdown, like the kind they do when a rocket is about to take off, or when you're ten seconds away from the new year. The birds are louder still, or I am stoned, and I do another leaf, *Bzeee-bzeee-bzeee-bzeee, Tsip, tsip, tsip, tit-tzeeeeee, Zray, zray zray zray sreeeeeee, Tsyoo-tsyoo-tsyoo-tsyoo-tswee, Zeeeeeeeeeeeeeee-tsyoo, Drink your teeeeee, towheee, Sweet, sweet, sweet, sweet-and-sweet,* and then I take out the lighter and somehow the path is on fire and I don't know if I meant it to be, and it goes up, and the birds scream, they scream at me, *Chip, chjjjj, chewk, Jaay and jaay-jaay notes, Tool-ool, tweedle-dee, chi-chuwee, what-cheer . . . Wheet, wheet, wheet, wheet. Chip, chjjjj, chewk, Jaay and jaay-jaay notes, Tool-ool, tweedle-dee, chi-chuwee, Tur-a-lee, Purdy purdy purdy . . . Whoit, whoit, whoit, whoit, what-cheer,* and before I can scream back, before the birds can take flight, it is up, sucking up the trees, with the sound of ice breaking, it goes up, and no amount of stamping will help, I can see that, I just watch it like I am part of it. The birds are loud and then it is just roar and I run for the rocks. Down the path I pass Denver who has sweat on his face in pearls. He roars as he passes but he doesn't stop to give me the beating of my life, he runs like murder into the fire and towards the Carter house, and I want to shout, *Stop, don't go that way!* but the sound of the birds and the noise of the fire roaring take the sound out of my mouth, and he goes into the hot trees, and I can't follow.

I swear I see a bird, bright and on fire, rise out of the trees and just keep on going up like it's a rocket going for Mars.

31

Lloyd fed the sheep, left me and Dog under a blanket on the sofa. I got up once he'd gone, and stood in front of the mirror and looked. My eyes blinked at me. I took off my bandage and underneath felt tender.

I washed my face, and then dipped my head in the sink, poured warm water over my hair with my cupped hand. The water ran out pink from the cut. I wrung out my hair and draped the hand towel over my shoulders. I opened the kitchen door and looked out at the hillside, then I closed the door, and leant the gun up next to it. I found the kitchen scissors and sat at the table to wait for Lloyd.

"What's this?" he said when he came in.

"I want you to cut my hair."

Lloyd was still for a moment looking at me, and then he came and stood behind me.

He pulled his fingers lightly through my hair.

He worked in silence, and lengths of hair dropped in my lap and crept down my back, and his fingers at the nape of my neck and at my temples were warm. I kept my eyes closed, and listened to the clean sound of the scissors.

After a long time, Lloyd put them down, laid his hands on my shoulders and said, "I'm so sorry. I've made you look so much worse. We're going to have to find a hairdresser's."

In the truck, Lloyd wrote a shopping list. "Shall we have some wine?" he asked. "I feel like I've overdone the whisky lately."

"I'm not going to a hairdresser," I said.

"Oh, come on. You need to go."

"It doesn't bother me. You can have another go later on if it makes you feel better."

"It won't make me feel better—it won't make you look better."

"It doesn't worry me. I don't feel worried by it."

"God almighty, you look more like a local than the locals do. I can't live with seeing this disaster I've created every day."

"It'll grow out. I can wear a hat."

"Wait," said Lloyd in a new voice. I pressed the brake but didn't stop.

"What?"

"Stop the car, stop the car." He turned to the back window and pressed his hand against the glass. I pulled into the lay-by.

"What is it?" Before the truck had properly stopped, Lloyd was outside. I slid out too, shutting Dog in—he panted in fury. Lloyd had crossed the road and started to move into the woods.

"Lloyd!" I called and he just held up one hand to silence me. I followed him, through the sticks and brambles, Dog yipping in the truck behind me. When I got closer, I saw Lloyd's cheek was bleeding where a branch had whipped him. He ploughed on; my ankle turned down a rabbit hole while I tried to keep up with him, the back of his jacket moving in and out of sunlight.

"Stop," I hissed, not sure what I was being quiet for. He stopped dead. When I caught up he was still apart from the breath which moved his back up and down, and which puffed around him like smoke.

I swallowed. "What is it?" I stood next to him and he put his finger to his lips and then pointed into the newly unfurled bracken.

"I see it," he whispered, and I looked and saw a shadow beneath the green canopy, where maybe something moved.

"What do you see?"

"It's huge," he said in a voice that did not sound like his own. "It's here—it's just here."

"And you see it?"

"It's just in front of us."

Something crunched in the undergrowth.

"Should we run?" I said, but I didn't think we would.

It moved deeper into the woods and we stayed standing, watching and listening.

"My god," said Lloyd quietly.

I looked down and saw that we were holding hands.

32

On the beach at low tide after a storm, the sharks that have washed up are the small ones that don't need to be towed onto the sand spit first. They are just finned on the boats and plopped back into the drink. There is a blue with its long and pointed snout, looking like a worm without its fins, and I squint at it trying to imagine it swimming, ever.

Soon I will go home, and there'll be Mum squirting cream into her drink. The place will smell of chip fat and laundry. Iris will be out the back in her version of a bikini, and the triplets will be complaining that tea is too far off and that what they need is chocolate milk, even though there is never any chocolate milk in our fridge. Dad will pull up in his car and there'll be the sound of him dropping his keys on the kitchen sideboard. I might ask for a dog again, just to join in. Dad opens the fridge and takes out a beer and it hisses open and this is how life will always be, and I will always be here.

Acknowledgements

Thank you to Mary Morgan and the Hereford sheep farmers who generously let me watch them at work and ask boring questions. Also to Sally, Pig and Sir Colin McColl for looking after me so well.

To Nikki Christer and all at Vintage Australia, and all at Pantheon in the U.S. for their hard work and very helpful edits. Special massive thanks to Diana Miller.

To everyone at Jonathan Cape and Mulcahy Associates, particularly Alex Bowler, Joe Pickering and my agent Laetitia Rutherford, for their exceptional skills and for being such kind friends.

Thanks Mum and Dad, Tom, Emma, Flynn, Jack, Matilda, Juno and Hebe, Roz, Roy and Gus.

Thanks Jamie for dealing with me and also for helping me write.